The Billionair

Billionaire Br

Penelope Ryan

Lilly: *I know that to him, I'm nothing more than a notch in his bedpost. He's the richest man in Seattle who can get any girl he wants. And I'm just one in a long line of conquests.*

There's only one problem. I'm falling in love. And to make matters worse ... I'm considering giving him my v-card.

Aiden: *I never thought I'd be the kind of man to settle for just one woman. But there's something about her that's pulling me in. There's never been a challenge I can't conquer, and her rejection is driving me wild. I'm more than infatuated. I'm obsessed.*

As a founder of a premiere Seattle tech company, Aiden King is no stranger to getting what he wants. Whether that be private jets, the best clothes, or the prettiest woman in the room. That's why, when his brother and cofounder assigns him to oversee one of their nonprofits, Aiden scoffs at the idea. Surely, his talents could be better utilized elsewhere. But, ever the team player, he sucks it up and agrees.

But on his first day on the job, he realizes it might not be as much of a slog as he'd thought. He'll be shadowing the program manager—a young, beautiful blonde with a feisty personality he can't resist. And her disinterest in him is only fueling his resolve.

Lilly Richards has never had much time for boyfriends. She's too busy dedicating her life to the Seattle youth community. And Aiden King—no matter how rich and handsome he is—is no exception.

But Aiden is used to getting what he wants. And he'll stop at nothing to make her his.

This story is a work of fiction. Any references to real events, people, or places are used fictitiously. Other names, events, characters, or places are a product of the author's imagination and any resemblance to actual names, events, people, or places is completely coincidental.

Copyright 2024 by Penelope Ryan

Chapter 1

Aiden

I step out into the brisk, autumn chill of the parking garage, wrapping my scarf tighter around my neck as I hurry to my car. It's a brand-new Porsche, in a shiny black. Even parked next to the various other luxury cars—owned by the other tenants in the upscale apartment complex I live in—I still think it stands out. A classic. You can't beat a Porsche.

Glancing hurriedly at the time as I settle into the driver's seat, I hiss in frustration under my breath. I'm late. I can only hope Asher isn't keeping a brotherly eye on me. I pull out of the garage and into the busy streets of downtown Seattle.

As an older brother, Asher isn't all that bad. He does most of the running of King Technologies—the company that he, I, and our other brother Alec—founded. In fact, up until very recently, his job was the only thing he cared about.

I'll admit, with his laser focus on the job, it's allowed me to take a bit of a backseat in recent years. Of course I was just as involved earlier when we were starting the company. But once the money started rolling in and things were able to simply run on autopilot, let's say I took a bit of a break to enjoy some of the finer things in life.

Traveling, going out, having fun. You know, the kind of stuff money should be spent on, right? In all honesty, I took Asher's laser focus on work for granted.

And now, he's ... let's just say *less* focused.

That's what love will do to you, I guess.

Olivia Reilly is her name. An assistant like no other. The first change I noticed in him was his overall personality. A bit less of an asshole, if I'm honest. If all it took was a girlfriend to make my brother more tolerable, I would have pushed for one years ago. Although I doubt just any girlfriend would've done it.

And she's more than a girlfriend now. A fiancée, as of six months ago. It's crazy how time flies. And the wedding is right around the corner.

The only problem is that the more time Asher spends with Olivia, the less time he spends on work. Meaning, I have to finally pick up some slack.

It's fair, if I'm honest with myself. I've been out of commission for way too long. So it's not like I can argue with the logic of Asher sitting me down last week and asking—demanding?—that I be more involved with the company. It is a third mine, after all.

"There's only so much I can do on my own," Asher had said to me from across his desk, glancing surreptitiously at his phone. The slight uptick in the corner of his mouth was a telltale sign the text was from Olivia. God, this guy has really fallen. "And you know Alec already takes on way more than he can handle."

It's true. Our brother Alec is a workaholic if there ever was one.

I'd felt that tiny smidgen of guilt that sometimes wormed its way through me when I thought of how little I'd given to the business in recent years. "What would help the most?"

Asher had obviously given it some thought because he came back with a quick answer. "The Maria King Foundation."

I'd simply blinked back at him. "What about it?"

Maria King. Our mom. She'd died when the three of us were all teenagers. A rare form of cancer that took her quicker than any of us were ready for. Since building our company—and swimming in more money than anyone could possibly know what to do with— we'd opened up a foundation in her name. An artist her whole life, we'd set up the nonprofit in her name to lead art therapy sessions, community workshops, and youth programs for kids and young people in the Seattle area. It's only been up and running for about two years, and truthfully, I never give it much thought.

"I need you to just check in on it," Asher had confided. "We set it up a few years ago and I have had no time to go through the books and see whether this foundation is able to stay afloat on its own and whether it seems to be making a real difference in terms of outreach."

"You doubt whether it's profitable?"

Asher snorted. "It's not supposed to be profitable, but *is* supposed to be a worthy allocation of funds. That's what I want you to look into. Is the foundation making a difference, and is that difference worth the money that we're putting into it?"

I'd agreed, no matter how boring it sounded. It's about time I make up for the years of playing around and neglecting the business. Not that I'm going to stop playing around, mind you.

I smile, thinking back to last night. The girl I'd picked up at a bar downtown. How I'd taken her back to my apartment and had my way with her on the dining room table, the couch, my bed. Her delicious moans are still ringing in my ears.

Fuck. Yeah, I'm not about to give up having fun anytime soon.

A sudden red light up ahead has me slamming on my breaks, bringing the car to a sudden halt. The coffee in my cupholder beside me lurches forward, spilling dark brown liquid across the console and my knees.

"Shit," I snap, hissing as it burns through my dress pants. "Shit, shit, shit."

I grit my teeth as I continue driving, knowing the car is going to smell awful at the end of the day. I'll have to get it detailed this weekend.

Looking down at the GPS on my phone, I see I'm only a few blocks away. I'm in a calmer part of Seattle now. The buildings aren't as high, the streets aren't as dense. After a few more turns, I reach what I assume to be the nonprofit headquarters. It's a modest-looking building. Not big, but not small either. A parking lot sits in front of it, and I pull in, taking a moment to try and dry myself off with a pair of napkins I find in my glove compartment.

Giving up with a huff, I step out of the car. A buzz has me glancing down at my phone to see a notification from Ben, my personal assistant. He handles most of my duties at King Tech all on his own—as well as informing me of meetings, deadlines, and other responsibilities. Today, it's a text about who I'm supposed to be meeting this morning.

Lilly Richards. The program manager. Ben tells me she's in charge of most of the day-to-day operations and that shadowing her will give me the best insight into the nonprofit's workings.

I shove my phone into my pocket and trudge across the rainy pavement up to the front doors.

I step inside, glancing around the shabby lobby decorated with various artworks, obviously all done by children. Handprints with smiley faces, green trees, sunflowers.

"Hello," a voice calls me out of my perusal.

I look forward to see a young woman seated at reception. She has brown hair, red glasses, and a nice smile. "Aiden King, right?" she asks.

I force a smile on my face. "Yes, that's me," I say, taking a step forward.

"Hi, I'm Monica. Lilly's expecting you," she says simply, standing from her seat. "Follow me."

I follow her down a hallway to the right, the floor covered in an old, brown carpet. She stops at a door on her right, swinging it open and calling, "Lilly? Mr. King is here."

She turns back to me, ushers me inside, and then leaves.

I walk into the small office. Various art prints line the walls, and behind a modest desk sits a woman who I presume is Lilly Richards. I stare at her in surprise, caught off guard. She's young. Younger than I thought a program manager at a nonprofit would be. She can't be much older than twenty-five.

And holy shit is she hot.

Her long blonde hair falls just below her breasts, and her soft brown eyes assess me from across the room.

"Mr. King," she says, standing and holding out her hand across her desk. "I'm Lilly Richards."

Mr. King. Those words coming from her mouth set a fire in my stomach. I step forward, taking her hand in mine and shaking it. It's warm and soft. "Nice to meet you," I say with a smile. She pulls her hand away first.

"Likewise."

As she leans forward to take her seat, a hint of cleavage peaks out beneath her white button-up blouse. I bite my lip, averting my gaze just in time for her not to notice.

When her eyes meet mine, I simply smile.

Fuck. Stepping up my work might not be so bad after all.

Chapter 2

Lilly

Aiden King is surprisingly attractive. I don't know exactly what I was expecting. Someone ... nerdier, I guess? We all know about the King brothers around here. I mean, King Tech funds us. But when you think of three brothers starting a tech company, you don't exactly imagine them as Abercrombie models.

I lock my jaw, resisting the urge to shake my head. *Snap out of it, Lilly*, I chide myself.

"Your assistant, Ben, filled me in on your goal here," I continue. "You're wanting to evaluate the Maria King Foundation for its worthiness." The words come out a bit harsher than I intended, and with my blank expression, it probably packs a punch. But I can't help it.

I think back to getting the email from Ben Holmes in my inbox a week ago. Aiden King would be shadowing the foundation for an indefinite amount of time to check up on operations. It was worded kindly, but I could read between the lines. They're doubting whether the foundation is worth keeping up. It's hard not to bristle when your job—and a good chunk of your personal identity—is threatened.

Aiden raises his eyebrows ever so slightly, the hint of a smirk fluttering across his face. It sends a spark of anger through me. He's amused? He's amused at the possibility of me losing my job? At the possibility of this foundation no longer helping the community?

"I wouldn't put it in those terms exactly," he says.

"Oh?" I fold my arms across my chest, leaning back in my chair. "What words would you ascribe to it then?"

He levels me with another amused gaze, which only makes me madder. I try my best to hide it.

"We're simply checking in on a foundation that our company funds. That's it."

I grit my teeth, trying to wipe any unpleasant expression off my face. I don't believe him for one minute, but a combative attitude on my part isn't going to help the situation.

I stand from my desk. "Let me show you around a bit. I've also set up an office for you."

I stride toward the door, brushing past him in the small room. The door across from my office used to be a storage space. We'd keep old art supplies and chairs in there. I've moved most of the larger things to various other closets throughout the building, and I found an old desk to take its place. I swing the door open and let Aiden enter.

He steps inside, a slight frown of displeasure on his face. I can't help but feel satisfied by his disappointment. "This is your office for the time being," I state.

He purses his lips, nodding slowly. "You can't move some of this stuff?" he eventually asks, gesturing to the piles of canvasses in the corner, along with a few folding chairs.

I raise my eyebrows. "Your stay here is temporary, correct?"

"I suppose," he relents.

"And you're welcome to find other places for them if they bother you that much."

He seems surprised that I'd suggest he do the work himself. I wonder when he last had to do any kind of manual labor. By the looks of him, probably quite a while ago.

"Maybe we can have an office decorating party," he suggests with a smile, cocking his head playfully.

"You can rearrange your office later," I say curtly, turning on my heel and sauntering down the hallway, not even glancing behind me to make sure he's following. I hear the pattering of his footsteps after me.

This hallway leads to a much larger one, with classrooms on either side. I gesture to them as we pass. "This is where we hold workshops and classes. Most are youth oriented, but a few are for adults as well." It's a Monday morning, so the classrooms are currently empty. Most of them are held in the afternoons and evenings.

"What kind of classes are they?" Aiden asks as we walk.

"Acrylic and watercolor painting are the most popular ones, but we have a huge variety of art mediums we teach here. We're even starting a pottery class next semester." I'd been pushing to get pottery approved basically since I started working here last year. With the expensive kilns and materials—not to mention a qualified teacher—it had felt like an uphill battle. But we'd finally gotten everything sorted, and I'm so excited for the class to debut in the fall.

"Pottery," Aiden muses. "Sexy."

Shocked, I shoot him a perplexed look over my shoulder. "Hardly."

He smirks. "What? You've never seen *Ghost*?"

I bristle in annoyance, knowing what he's getting at. Instead of dignifying his comments with a response, I simply keep walking.

I show Aiden around the rest of the building—a handful of classrooms, administrative offices, a lunchroom, and then I bring him back to our offices.

I shoot him a tight-lipped smile. "Let me know if I can do anything for you while you're here." I turn to head back into my office when Aiden stops me.

"Could you get me a record of the foundation's expenses? Along with any incoming money, funds raised, etc.?"

"Sure. I'll email you the files." I nod curtly. "I can also send over some of our promotional materials. You know, success stories, kids who have gone on to college, kids who we've helped with the scholarship program—"

"Just the expenses should be fine," Aiden says with a wave of his hand.

He turns to head into his office, when I stop him, frustrated. "You know, the foundation is more than just numbers on a piece of paper. Looking at just the numbers, you won't see the impact we've had on the community. We've helped so many people. We're more than an expense record." I feel my voice rising, and I force myself to cut it off. Blowing up at him won't help. I lock my jaw and take a deep breath, leveling him with a gaze that I'm hoping is confident yet stern.

That stupid smirk returns to Aiden's face. A smirk I'm becoming all too familiar with. "I'll be the judge of that," he says simply and walks into his office.

I spin on my heel and make my way to my desk, burying my head in my hands. I take a few deep breaths. While I hadn't known exactly what to expect from Aiden King, I sure hadn't expected this. Not a cocky, young asshole who obviously isn't taking this as seriously as he should.

I bite my lip, staring off to the side at the wall where a variety of kids' drawings litter the drywall. I've had a myriad of dreams over the years, and when I landed this job a year ago, I never dreamed it would turn into what it has. A job that's given me purpose, a real mission.

After being here for a year and seeing exactly what this foundation does for kids in this community, I'm more determined than ever to prove to the Kings that it's worth keeping up. Whatever Aiden King decides about the Maria King Foundation, I'm certainly not going down without a fight.

Chapter 3

Aiden

I can see her through the two windows in our office doors. Sitting right across the hall from each other, our desks are both facing outward, and if I crane my neck in just the right angle, I can catch a glimpse of her long, blonde hair and the side of her face.

Lilly. Lilly Richards. Quite possibly the prettiest girl I've ever seen. Not done up in some cocktail dress and a face full of makeup like the girls I meet at the bar. No. After the few days I've known her, I've seen her come to work in jeans and simple blouses. Her hair looks natural—no curling or styling, it simply falls in light waves down her back. And her makeup is simple. Maybe some mascara?

And to my shock, I've never wanted someone more.

Conquests have never really been difficult for me. Maybe that's why this Lilly girl is so appealing. She's so uninterested. Hostile, even. But fuck, if I could only get her to change her mind …

I shake my head, trying to rid myself of improper thoughts and get my mind back on work. I've spent the last few days going through the expense reports and getting a good idea of the overall financial situation of the foundation. So far, it seems pretty standard.

I lean back from my laptop, needing a break from the screen. I glance around the room. Despite what Lilly had suggested, I had not taken the time to remove the various art supplies and furniture from my temporary office. After all, she was right. My stay here is temporary. A few weeks at most, I'm assuming.

Although, I suppose that's up to Asher in the end.

I see quite a few canvasses piled up against the walls, and a few in the corner catch my eye. Unlike the others, these look painted on. I stand and make my way over to them, pulling them away from the wall to glance down at the front side.

I cock my head to get a better view. Landscapes, by the look of it. But brightly colored and beautifully executed. I frown. Is this the kind of art they teach these kids here? I've never been much of an art guy, but even I have to admit that this is stunning. I purse my lips. Maybe Lilly has a point after all. Maybe this foundation really does some good.

Mom would be glad to hear it.

I don't spend much time thinking about her. It's hard, in all honesty. Her death was a surprise, and it hit us all hard. The youngest of my brothers, I'd been thirteen when she'd died. And while I obviously know it was hard for everyone, I felt like I'd taken it the hardest. Mom and I had been close. We'd had a special bond. And losing her at that age had killed me.

Dad had grown distant after that, and from then on, no one in our family really discussed her. My brothers and I set up this organization a few years ago in her name, but even then, we rarely discussed her except for the idea of naming the foundation after her.

And now, staring down at the artwork leaned against the floor, I can't help the flood of memories. I push it back against the wall abruptly and hurry back to my desk. Now isn't the time for sentimentalities. It's never the time for that, really. What good will it do? Sitting in sadness won't bring her back.

Sitting back down in front of my laptop, my mind wanders back to Lilly. Things have been tense since I got here on Monday. She seems pretty intent on disliking me. Why, I'm unsure. Well, I suppose because she thinks I'm here to shut down the foundation. Put her out of a job. I guess that's a fair reason. Although that's not my intent. I mean, if I think the foundation is bleeding money with no real added value, I'll be honest about it with Asher and Alec, but I have no ill will toward it.

I glance down at the time on the bottom of my laptop screen. It's almost the end of the day.

I spend the next hour going through a few more files, taking notes to go through later.

When five o'clock rolls around, I barely notice it. What I do notice is a flash of blonde hair and the sound of a door shutting. I glance up to see Lilly closing her office door and strutting down the hallway.

Without even thinking, I leap up from my chair and dash to the door, swinging it open into the hallway.

"Lilly," I call, and she whirls around, a look of surprise painted across her pretty face. "Is it the end of the day already?" I ask with a chuckle, glancing down at my phone.

She snorts. "Yeah. A little after five." She shifts her bag over her shoulder. "How's everything going with the reports? I haven't seen much of you today."

I warm at the slight interest. At least she's not trying to run for the hills. Besides, if it were up to me, I'd be seeing a whole lot of her today and every day. I shrug nonchalantly. "Boring. But that's to be expected."

She purses her lips. "Yeah, I told you the numbers aren't what matters here."

She turns, but before she can take a step, I blurt out, "How do you feel about grabbing a drink?"

She looks back at me, and I can see the refusal bubbling up within her.

"You can tell me more about how the foundation helps all those kids," I say quickly. And just as I knew it would, that gets to her. Her gaze softens, and I can see her contemplating the offer in her mind. After a few seconds of narrowed eyes, she finally relents.

"Okay," she says softly. "But just one drink."

Chapter 4

Lilly

What the hell am I thinking? I pull up to the bar just a short drive from work. Aiden had suggested it, and I'd plugged the address into Google maps. I sit in my car for a minute, waiting for him to pull in behind me. I roll my eyes in exasperation at myself. Why the hell did I agree to this?

Of course I've gone out for drinks or dinner with coworkers from time to time. I'm not opposed to the idea of getting to know the people you work with. But there's something about Aiden King that feels … dangerous? I don't know. That's probably an over exaggeration.

But it's not like we can truly have a casual working relationship. He's one of the founders of King Tech, where the foundation gets all its money from. And regardless of what he says, I know the only possible reason he's there is because someone at the company has doubts about the Maria King Foundation. What those doubts are, I don't know. I'd been infuriated when I'd first been informed of Aiden's coming to oversee the foundation. It's an incredible place, and it does a lot.

So, no matter how nice we play, Aiden poses a real threat to my job. To the foundation I've poured my heart and soul into.

Does he not see that?

It appears not, based on that stupid, goofy smile he's been sending my way all week. I'm not an idiot. His flirting has not been lost on me. And honestly, under other circumstances, maybe I'd give him a shot. He is, I have to admit, attractive. His hair is dark and slightly wavy, and he has this five o'clock shadow that somehow still makes him look put together and manicured.

Aiden waves at me through the window of my car, pulling me from my daze. I grab my purse off the passenger seat and hop out. I shoot him a tight-lipped smile before following him inside the bar.

It's a nice place. An upscale restaurant with an extensive cocktail menu. Not exactly the kind of place I was expecting. I do most of my socializing in dive-bar-type establishments.

The restaurant is pretty busy, so we opt for seats at the long bar that stretches across almost the entirety of the main room. Fancy spirits and liquors line shelves along the wall. Aiden settles in, leaning his elbows against the countertop and flagging down a bartender.

"A gin and tonic," he says, then gestures to me.

I stutter for a moment, not quite sure what I want, then I answer, "A cabernet if you have it."

The bartender nods and heads off.

We sit in an awkward silence for a few heartbeats. I fidget in my seat, glancing around. I feel Aiden's gaze on me, and I turn to see that familiar smile on his face. Almost like a smirk. Like he's amused about something. It sends a wave of frustration through me. What the hell is he smiling about?

Even more annoying, he seems able to read my mind, because he chuckles. "You seem irritated," he observes. But instead of looking worried over that fact, he simply seems entertained.

I resist the urge to roll my eyes. The bartender returns then with our drinks, setting them in front of us and then hurrying away.

I grasp my glass of wine, bringing it to my lips in order to avoid an answer.

"Am I really that annoying?" Aiden presses, his smile growing.

I sigh quietly. "You're not annoying."

He raises an eyebrow. "Oh? Then what's with the attitude?"

I widen my eyes. Did he really just say that? What the hell is wrong with this guy? "I—I have no idea what you're talking about," I stutter.

He chuckles again. "Oh, come on. You think I haven't noticed the cold shoulder you've been giving me ever since I arrived?"

"It's called professionalism, maybe you should take notes." The minute the words leave my lips, I realize how harsh they sound, and I'm suddenly worried. After all, Aiden could get me fired on the spot if he wanted to. But that worry is quickly replaced by irritation again when he throws his head back and laughs.

I purse my lips, staring down at my glass of wine.

"You are professional, I'll give you that," Aiden says. "Very dedicated to your job, it seems."

"Is that a bad thing?"

"Of course not." He shakes his head. "Just an observation."

"I care deeply about the work I do," I clarify. "Those art workshops can change kids' lives. Give them things to look forward to, skills—making them happy. It's important."

Aiden pauses for just a second before nodding. "I see your point. I mean, it's why we set up the foundation in the first place. Look, I'm not the bad guy here." He holds out his hands in surrender.

I unclench my jaw. Maybe I should go easier on him. Maybe he's right.

"My presence doesn't necessarily mean bad things for the foundation."

But that word nags at the back of my mind. *Necessarily*. He's not promising anything.

"Tell me about you," Aiden surprises me by saying. He leans forward against the bar, taking a sip of his gin and tonic.

"Me?" I repeat hollowly.

He snorts, that dumb smirk returning to his face. "Yes, you. Tell me about yourself."

I raise my eyebrows. "Well, I work at your foundation. I've lived in Seattle all my life. I …"

Aiden cuts me off, rolling his eyes. "I didn't ask for a work bio. How about what you do for fun. Do you have a boyfriend?"

I widen my eyes slightly. "No. No boyfriend," I answer.

Aiden's eyes light up a bit at that, and I resist the urge to narrow my eyes.

"How does a girl who looks like you not have a boyfriend?"

Okay, I can't resist it anymore. I roll my eyes. Although a tiny part of me warms at his words. I can only hope I'm not noticeably blushing. Fuck. He's obviously a player. What the hell is wrong with me? "Maybe it's the lack of acceptable men," I quip.

"Disappointing, huh?"

"Very."

"Well, I can't say *I've* ever left a woman disappointed," Aiden murmurs with a smirk. He leans toward me. "They've all been very, *very* satisfied." His voice is low, and his gaze is locked on mine, seemingly pinning me to my seat. There's something in his look that sets a fire low in my belly. A fire that I'm trying my hardest to quickly extinguish.

I take a deep breath, breaking our gaze and shifting on the stool. Why did Aiden King have to be so goddamn handsome? Those stupidly blue eyes and that chiseled jaw. Fuck.

"That's very … fun for you," I manage to reply, trying to keep my cool. I take a sip of wine nonchalantly.

He shrugs. "I think it's more fun for them."

I laugh, looking anywhere but directly at him.

"You think I'm joking?" I can tell by his tone that he's grinning.

God damn it, I can feel a hot flush creeping across my neck. I hope Aiden can't see it. I force myself to look at him and portray an unmoved expression. I purse my lips. "Not to question your expertise, but men are notorious for not exactly knowing the different between a performance and the real thing," I answer casually.

A shocked laugh bubbles up from his chest. He sets his glass down on the bar, leaning over slightly and laughing. "Lilly Richards," he says after a moment, and my name on his lips sends another round of butterflies through my stomach. "You're funny."

I can't tell if I'm more infuriated by the fact that he's simply laughing at my intended insult, or at the fact that I'm shockingly, irritatingly, unacceptably drawn to that stupid smile on his face. That my name coming out of his mouth was the best sound I've heard all day.

Aiden composes himself, his hand now on the back of my seat, his body closer to me than he's been all night. His eyes are still twinkling from my apparently hilarious comeback. "But if you're wanting to test your theory, I'd be more than happy to play along," he says quietly.

Heat pools in my core at his words, his proximity, the heat of his hand softly brushing against my back. Fuck. No, no, no. I swallow.

"I ..." I stammer. I glance at our glasses on the bar. Practically gone. We've been here long enough. And I did only promise him one drink. And I'm afraid if I stay any longer, I might ...

"I should probably go," I decide aloud, tugging my jacket off my chair, which roughly removes Aiden's hand. I hop off the stool, grabbing my purse. "Thanks for the drink," I say, assuming that he'll pay up before he leaves.

And with one quick glance at his surprised expression, I turn on my heel and leave.

Chapter 5

Aiden

I sit at the bar in stunned silence watching the last flash of blonde hair as Lilly escapes through the front door. My mouth slightly ajar, my brow furrowed, I slowly turn back to the bar, grasping my gin and tonic in my hand.

What just happened?

I'm almost too stunned to process the fact that I was just … rejected? No, that can't be. I almost want to laugh out loud. I can't remember the last time a girl turned me down. Back in high school, maybe? I wrack my brain. Sure, girls play coy. They pretend they aren't interested, they play hard to get. But flat out rejection?

Wow, that's a foreign feeling. Jesus Christ, have I lost my edge?

I chuckle, still in shock, then take a sip of my drink. Lilly Richards. The prettiest woman I've ever seen, and the first woman I've encountered who *doesn't* want to sleep with me. Some cruel, cosmic joke, it seems.

But instead of frustration, defeat, or even a sense of failure, a completely different emotion surfaces. Determination. She might have stormed out of here pretending she was disgusted with me, but I'm experienced enough to read a woman. I'd noticed that faint blush creeping up her neck, the way she'd look anywhere but directly at me. The way her gaze had lingered on my lips just a second too long. She isn't as uninterested as she's pretending to be.

I shake my head. Lilly Richards might just be the first girl to turn me down, but I'm not giving up without a fight.

Chapter 6

Lilly

I twirl my fork aimlessly through my Caesar salad, smiling in greeting when Monica enters the breakroom, lunch in hand.

"Crazy day," Monica mutters, setting her lunch bag on the small table and sitting down across from me. The door to the breakroom swings shut behind her with a soft click.

I nod, widening my eyes. "That pottery workshop is turning out to be a pain to organize." I'd been so excited about it—and still am—but the kilns aren't ready yet, we've been having shipping problems with the supplies, and the teacher is seemingly less available than she'd originally told us. Ugh.

"We should do something fun this weekend to get our minds off work," Monica says, pulling out her sandwich and taking a bite. Monica and I both started here at the same time, about a year ago, and we've been friends ever since. We're roughly the same age—Monica is twenty-two, and I'm twenty-four.

"There's a cute flea market I keep hearing about on Capitol Hill," I suggest.

"Ooooh, yes," Monica agrees. She glances around, looking over my shoulder and presumably through the glass window on the breakroom door to make sure no one's around. She leans toward me, a mischievous smile on her face. I already know what she's going to say, and I'm chuckling in preparation. "So, Aiden King." She widens her eyes at me. We haven't had a moment alone since he arrived early this week. "*Cute.*" She shakes her head. "God, I didn't expect him to be that cute."

I roll my eyes. "I suppose."

"You suppose?" Monica repeats. "Are you blind?"

I laugh. "Okay, okay." There's no use in pretending. Not with Monica anyway. Besides, I barely made it out of that bar last night without doing something I'd surely regret. I'm still in disbelief that it actually happened. Sure, I'd kind of assumed his invitation to get drinks would lead to some flirting— but blatantly suggesting we sleep together? My god. I hadn't really expected that. Although, based on his actions so far, I wonder if that was naïve. He's definitely made his intentions clear. And maybe if circumstances were different, I'd take him up on it. I mean, he'd practically dared me to …

"Earth to Lilly," Monica says, laughing when I shake my head and focus my attention back on her.

"Sorry," I say.

She smirks. "Daydreaming about Mr. King?"

I laugh then lean forward conspiratorially. There was never a chance I wasn't going to tell Monica about what happened last night. She'd kill me if I didn't. "Speaking of Mr. King, you'll never guess what happened last night."

Monica widens her eyes. "Holy shit. You didn't."

"No! God. No." I laugh, glancing over my shoulder to ensure no one's around. "But oh did he try." I widen my eyes in emphasis.

Monica's mouth drops open, a delighted smile spreading across her face. Giggling, I tell her about how he'd suggested we get drinks, his flirting, and his very obvious innuendos.

"Man, you have much more self-control than I do," Monica says with a laugh. "I'd have taken him up on that offer."

"Oh please," I say.

She raises an eyebrow at me. "I'm sure his offer still stands."

I open my mouth in shock. "Monica, I'm *not* going to sleep with Aiden King."

"And why not?" she shoots back.

"Maybe because he's technically our boss? The man who holds the future of the foundation in his hands?" And maybe one more reason that no one else knows about. Not even her.

"You know, I suspect that sleeping with him would only improve our chances of survival," Monica muses with a devilish grin.

I burst into laughter. "Well, I'm not about to test that theory."

She chuckles, pausing to take a bite of her sandwich. When she's finished chewing, she asks, "How has dating life been, by the way?" She levels me with a curious look.

I sigh. How has my dating life been? An absolute wasteland, if I'm honest.

"So, nobody?" Monica guesses after my hesitation.

I take a deep breath, shaking my head. "You know me. The time and effort that goes into dating? All for the risk of just breaking your heart?" I scoff. "Is it even worth it?"

She purses her lips. "It's obviously worth it, Lilly."

I grimace. I suppose she's right. I mean, everyone dates. And it's not like I've never dated. I have. I've just never really had a relationship that turned into anything. A relationship that lasted. I guess I'm just too scared. Too scared of getting my heart broken, of falling in love and being torn to pieces. It's also why I've never …

Well. That doesn't matter.

Sensing that the subject is somewhat sore, Monica quickly moves on, suggesting a coffee shop in Capitol Hill that we should try out before the flea market on Saturday. I nod along, looking forward to the weekend but still somewhat caught up in thoughts of dating and, surprisingly, Aiden.

If ever there was a man I'd want to date, he'd be the one. Perfectly sculpted jaw, a stupidly handsome smile. Too bad it's too risky. Too bad I'm still too scared. And too bad I'm … well, never mind. Too bad, is all.

Chapter 7

Aiden

This glorified storage room masquerading as an excuse for an office is really starting to get on my nerves. I can barely move around without tripping over some box full of paints or a pile of canvasses. Too bad Lilly and I can't just share an office. I grin at the thought. That would be fun, wouldn't it? I could tease her all day and watch her face grow red when I'd say something especially flirty.

I think back to our night at the bar and how hot and bothered she'd seemed. Just thinking about it forces a smile across my face. She'd given me the cold shoulder the rest of the week, regardless of my attempts to engage her in conversation. She'd simply flit away after a one-word answer or avoid me entirely.

I'd spent the weekend trying to get her out of my head, trying not to think about the sway of her hips as she walks or the curve of her breasts in those tight blouses she wears. Fuck, I'm a goner. I'm infatuated. I'm obsessed. I can't stop thinking about her. And from experience, I know there's only one way to get her out of my mind—to get her underneath me.

A buzz from my phone catches my attention. Looking down, I see a text from Asher.

Asher: *Unsurprisingly, I see you never RSVP'd for the wedding.*

I snort. Shit. Asher and Olivia's wedding. I knew it was this month, but I can't quite remember when. Pulling up my calendar, I'm shocked to see it's barely five days away—it's this weekend. Worst brother in the world award right here. I shake my head.

Aiden: *Yeah, sorry. Oops. Obviously I'm coming, though. Think you could have deduced that.*

Asher responds right away.

Asher: *You have a plus one?*

I stare down at the screen. Hadn't really thought of that. I'd kind of hoped maybe there'd be a cute bridesmaid of Olivia's to hook up with. But then another thought occurs to me.

Aiden: *Maybe I'll bring the program manager.*

A few minutes go by, and Asher doesn't respond. He probably thinks I'm kidding. Which, honestly, I kind of was, but on second thought ... would she go for it? Weddings are a romantic affair, the perfect setting for a hookup. I might just get lucky. I text Asher again.

Aiden: *You didn't warn me about how hot she is. All I can think about is getting in her pants.*

That gets a response.

Asher: *Jesus Christ, Aiden.*

I chuckle, setting my phone down and getting back to work. A half hour ticks by. I'm still slogging my way through last year's expense reports on the foundation. It seems like we shelled out quite a bit of money early on, but the costs have leveled out as time goes on. Hopefully that's a pattern that continues into this year as well.

I take another break to rest my eyes from the computer glare and glance around my office again. I shake my head. If I'm going to be here for a little while—which, guessing by the amount of time it's taking me to go through all these files, might be some time—I need a more appealing office space. Call me entitled, but I enjoy an aesthetically pleasing environment.

I stand from my desk, saunter across my office, across the hall, and open Lilly's office door.

She looks up, surprised. She raises her eyebrows.

"Lilly," I say with a smile.

"Mr. King," she says slowly.

"God. Don't call me that," I say with a wave of my hand.

This gets a small smile from her. It sends a spark of excitement through me. "What do you want, Aiden?" she says.

I grin wider. "I want to know where I can dump all that crap in my office. I need to clear it out, it's bugging me."

"Crap?" she repeats. "You mean the various supplies we need in order to run this foundation?"

"Yes, that." I cross my arms and lean against the doorframe.

With a sigh, she stands from her desk. I quickly scan her body when she's not looking, my gaze lingering on her hips. When she straightens and walks toward me, I flit my gaze back to her face, smiling confidently.

She brushes past me and into my office. I follow her. She stands for a few seconds, glancing around. Finally, she says, "I can see how it's a bit distracting."

"Thank you," I say, holding my hands out. "It's overwhelming, all this stuff. Where can I move it?"

She shoots me a sidelong glance. "There's a classroom that's rarely used down at the end of the hall. We can store most of this in a corner or something."

She steps forward, reaching down to grab a few canvasses leaning against the wall. As she twirls with them, on her way to the door, I catch a flash of color and recognize them from the other day.

"Wait," I say, stopping her. "I actually like those. Can I put those up in here? There's nothing on the walls."

She pauses, her mouth partway open as if a rebuttal is on its way.

"Besides, shouldn't you be displaying the students' work? Those are beautiful pieces."

"Um, well ..." she stutters, and I can see a familiar blush creeping up her cheeks. Like the blush from the bar last week.

I shoot her a puzzled look.

She sighs, a small, embarrassed smile playing across her lips. "They're mine, actually."

I raise my eyebrows. "Yours?" I repeat. "As in, you painted those?"

She nods.

"They're incredible." I reach for the one closest to me, pulling it from her hand. It's a vibrant meadow filled with greens, reds, oranges, and yellows. It's summertime in the most colorful way. It's somehow nostalgic and new all at once. "I didn't know you painted."

She shrugs.

"You're ... very talented."

I glance up at her, and that blush has only deepened. If I was trying to flatter her, I'd be pleased with myself, but I'm honestly too shocked to even be thinking of that. These paintings are beautiful. And she made them. What the hell is she doing here? Organizing little workshops when she should be teaching them—or selling this stuff.

"Thank you," she says with a self-deprecating laugh. She brushes a strand of blonde hair behind her ear, looking anywhere but at me.

"So, are you okay if I put them up in here?" I ask her genuinely. "I mean, if you want them for something else, by all means, take them. But they should be displayed somewhere, not just sitting in a pile."

She stares at me for a few heartbeats before finally nodding. "Sure." A small smile returns to her face. "You're right, they should be ... used." She laughs softly.

We stand in an awkward silence for a few moments, a strange electricity burning through the air. "What are you doing this weekend?" I find myself asking before I even allow myself to consider whether it's a good idea.

She cocks her head. "I'm not sure," she stutters.

"Do you like weddings?"

Chapter 8

Lilly

Smoothing the skirt of my light blue, satin dress, I stare up at the mansion before me in awe. I'd doubt it was the actual wedding venue if it wasn't for the other elegantly dressed guests and the huge, hand-painted sign that reads "Asher and Olivia" on a stand outside the front door.

The grounds are meticulously manicured, and the lawn beside the enormous house stretches far into the distance, with chairs and a gorgeous wedding arch already set up and waiting. I can catch a glimpse of a tent on the other side of the house, presumably where the reception will take place. Ivy adorns the house, as well as the stone fencing surrounding the entire venue.

I wonder how much this venue alone must have cost. More than I'll ever be able to afford, for sure.

Nervous, I begin to doubt—yet again—why I'd agreed to attend this wedding with Aiden. The word "sure" had just popped out of my mouth right after he'd asked me. I'd barely given it any thought before I'd agreed. And here I am. Standing in front of one of the most lavish events I've ever seen, feeling wholly out of place.

I'd convinced myself that Aiden and I were simply going as colleagues. It is, somewhat, work related. I mean, Asher is also a founder of the company that runs the foundation. Aiden only asked to be polite. We're not here as … well, anything.

"Lilly!" a voice calls, accompanied by the warm brush of a hand on the small of my back.

I twirl to see Aiden, and a burst of butterflies flutter through my stomach. God, he looks incredible. He's wearing a suit and tie, his hair combed back, his blue eyes twinkling. His hand on my back suddenly feels red hot, all of my attention focused on it.

But just as quickly as he'd placed it there, it's gone. He ushers me toward the doors of the large mansion, and I follow him.

Inside, the décor is just as extravagant as what's outside. Large chandeliers hang from the ceiling, and bouquets and floral arrangements—in the wedding colors of light blue and white—adorn practically every surface.

A waiter offers us champagne, and Aiden accepts for both of us, handing me a glass. After taking a sip, he chuckles. "You look shellshocked," he comments.

"Oh." I shake my head. "Sorry. I've just never seen a wedding this …" I struggle for the right word. "Elaborate."

"Yeah, Asher felt the need to invite pretty much all of the Seattle elite, so …" He shrugs. "And he loves an excuse to throw a good party."

"Aiden," a deep voice says from behind us, and we both turn. A man with very similar features to Aiden claps him on the back in greeting. He's basically just a slightly taller, slightly older version of him. He has to be one of the other King brothers. Is it Asher?

The man shoots me a polite but questioning look, obviously expecting to be introduced.

"Lilly," Aiden says, "this is my brother Alec."

Alec reaches out a hand. "Nice to meet you, Lilly."

"She's the program manager at the foundation," Aiden elaborates.

Alec's face brightens. "Oh yes, Asher had said you were working on that." He turns to face me. "I'd been meaning to drop by the foundation ever since we started it up, but …" He throws his hands up in the air. "Alas." He chuckles. "It's wonderful to finally meet you. I'm so proud of how the foundation has been able to serve the Seattle community."

I smile in surprise, taken slightly aback by his enthusiasm. If Aiden had had just a fraction of this upon meeting him, I'm sure our first week wouldn't have been so rocky. "Thank you," I say. "The work really means a lot to me." I glance sideways at Aiden. "All I want is to be able to continue. I—we—have so many ideas for the foundation."

Alec's smile widens. "That's so great to hear. Please share those ideas with Aiden while he's with you guys. We'd love to be able to incorporate them." He nods in Aiden's direction.

Someone flags Alec's attention, and with a nod, he's off to mingle with a new set of guests. I stare after him in surprise. From what Alec had said, it certainly doesn't feel like the Maria King Foundation is on the chopping block. Or maybe he's just being nice. It is a family wedding, after all. Not exactly the time to be a bearer of bad news.

Aiden's staring at me with a strange look on his face, but before he can open his mouth, we're bombarded by a new group of guests. Friends of the brothers from high school, apparently. I'm introduced, and after that, it's a series of random introductions until an announcement is made to head to the ceremony area outside.

Following the crowd, I step out into the backyard where an array of white chairs are laid before us. An elaborately carved arch stands at the top of the aisle, covered in florals. I follow Aiden to the front row, where we sit next to Alec and an older man I assume to be their father. Glancing around, I feel self-conscious in the front row of a wedding where I haven't even met the bride and groom. But I hardly have time to dwell on that before a quartet of violins begins playing and Asher and his groomsmen take their places beside the arch.

As a procession of bridesmaids glide down the aisle, I fix my gaze on Asher. Just like Alec, he looks similar to Aiden, although slightly broader and with darker eyes. He fidgets with his cufflinks, switching his weight from foot to foot. I can't help but smile at his nerves. The readiness for what's to come.

When his face lights up, I turn to follow his gaze, and there is Olivia Reilly at the end of the aisle.

Her dress is magnificent. A cream satin with a simple tulle veil. She walks alone, gripping tightly to the bouquet of blue and white flowers in her hands. Her brown eyes sparkle with emotion, her lip quivering into a radiant smile the closer she gets.

When she reaches him, she hands her bouquet off to a bridesmaid, and Asher grips her hands tightly in his. He whispers something to her that only she can hear, and she laughs quietly. And with that, the officiant starts.

The vows are beautiful, and when they kiss, Asher grips Olivia's waist, pressing her against him in quite possibly the most passionate kiss I've ever seen. Hand in hand, they walk down the aisle to roaring applause, Olivia waving her bouquet in the air and Asher pumping his fist and laughing.

Swept up in the emotion, I find myself clapping and laughing along, following the crowd as we're ushered to the reception area, a large tent on the other side of the house with gorgeous tables and chairs, a large dancefloor, and twinkling lights draped between the house, the trees, and the tent.

Aiden and I are offered cocktails, and I find myself laughing along with the other guests, milling around and snacking on hors d'oeurvres until Asher and Olivia make their grand entrance and dinner is served, along with toasts that make everyone both laugh and cry.

I'm surprised when Aiden stands up beside me, taking the microphone handed to him by the MC, and gives a rousing, embarrassing speech about Asher's younger years. I can see him turning beet red and shaking his head while Olivia laughs in delight.

When they stand to begin their first dance, they twirl across the dance floor as if they're the only two people in the room, the music ringing in the air around them. Halfway through the song, the guests are encouraged to join in, and to my surprise, Aiden stands, tugging me with him.

I look at him questioningly.

He chuckles. "It's a wedding, Lilly. You have to dance."

I acquiesce, letting him pull me out onto the dance floor where he grasps my hand in his and reaches for my waist. His fingers send a shiver up my spine as they settle just above the curve of my hip. Looking down at me and meeting my gaze, he takes a confident step back, and I follow, swaying to the music.

Lost in those blue eyes of his, I find it harder and harder to look away. Those butterflies in my stomach are back. My entire body burns with electricity. I force my head to turn, glancing around the room. The only other couples on the dance floor seem to be real couples. Women leaning their heads on their partners' shoulders, couples kissing softly as they sway.

"You never mentioned you had ideas for the foundation," Aiden says softly, and my attention turns back to him.

"Didn't I?" I ask, my voice coming out quieter than I'd intended. I clear my throat.

He shakes his head. "What kind of ideas?"

I smile at him in amusement. "You want to talk work at your brother's wedding?"

His eyes are warm. "It's more than just work to you."

It's a statement, not a question. And I'm taken aback by how true it is. And not only that—he *knows* it's true. He knows me. "You're right," I say.

"So, tell me about your ideas." He holds me with his gaze, the other couples spinning around us.

"I ... I thought we could have art shows. Like real art shows. Go all out. Champaine, people dressed up—the whole nine yards. We can showcase an emerging artist. Help them get on their feet. Maybe even showcase students. And with your connections at King Tech, you could invite, well, *wealthy* people. It could be a real way to raise money for the foundation." When I realize I'm rambling, I stop short, looking to Aiden for some kind of reaction.

But to my surprise, he doesn't seem dismissive or skeptical. He seems ... intrigued.

He bites his lip in thought, his eyebrows furrowing. "That's actually …" He chuckles, shaking his head. "That's actually a good idea."

I laugh, feigning insult. "You're surprised I have a good idea?"

He smirks. "Not at all." He steps to the side, twirling me under his arm and then pulling me back to him. The momentum sends me closer than I was before, my chest brushing softly against his, our breaths intermingling. His hand on my waist holds me close, his body heat seeping into every inch of me. My breath hitches in my throat as I gaze up at him, his eyes intense with an emotion I can't quite identify.

Suddenly the song ends, causing couples to step back from each other, the chatter in the room slowly returning to normal. Aiden holds me against his chest for a few heartbeats before the next song comes on—something upbeat and catchy. He steps back, letting go of me, the spot on my back where his hand had been suddenly cold and empty.

I take a small step back as well, glancing around. "How does a drink sound?" Aiden asks, breaking the awkward tension suddenly between us.

I smile. "Perfect."

Chapter 9

Lilly

The venue has multiple open bars, and Aiden and I venture inside the mansion to where it's less crowded. Within a few minutes, the bartender hands us our drinks. I take a sip of mine—some custom couples cocktail Asher and Olivia had designed together for the event.

The room we're in has couches, chairs, a large fireplace, and tables for people to set drinks down on. A handful of people are lounging on some couches, drinks in hand, laughing.

I glance around the corner, seeing an ornately decorated hallway that passes a kitchen on the right and then leads to who knows where. My head on a swivel, I feel like I can't get enough of this place. Aiden notices my interest and raises an amused eyebrow at me.

I laugh. "This venue must have cost an arm and a leg."

Aiden smirks. "Well, if there's anything Asher has, it's 'arms and legs.' A lot of them."

I snort. "Not just Asher, I assume." I raise my eyebrows at him. "I mean, you and Alec are cofounders too, right?"

He shrugs, whether modestly or secretively, I can't quite tell. "You're not wrong," he admits.

I nod, continuing my perusal of the room—the chandeliers above us, the intricate carvings on the ceiling.

"You want to explore?" Aiden suggests.

I shoot him a quizzical look. "Can we?"

"If my brother paid an arm and a leg for this venue, then we'd better be able to explore it if we want. Come on." Wrapping his arm around mine, he tugs me down the hallway.

"Interesting décor choice," I comment, gesturing to an array of portraits on the walls. The subjects look older—from medieval times, perhaps?—with long, sad faces and eyes that follow as you walk by.

"For real," Aiden agrees. "Whatever happened to fields of daises?"

Suddenly we pass an open doorway to our left. Aiden stops short, peering inside. He makes a soft noise of interest, taking a step in. I follow. The room appears to be a library of sorts. Bookshelves line the walls, and a warm fireplace burns in the corner, surrounded by a chaise lounge and a few chairs.

"Cute," I comment, walking around.

Aiden walks to the nearest bookshelf, brushing his fingers along the spines.

I gravitate toward the fireplace, taking a seat on the chaise lounge and staring into the embers. "How did Asher and Olivia meet?" I ask over my shoulder.

"Olivia was his personal assistant," Aiden responds behind me.

"Mmmm, a workplace romance."

Aiden chuckles. "Incredibly improper coming from Asher." I hear him come up behind me, and then he takes a seat next to me on the lounge. Our thighs barely brush, and a streak of electricity runs through me.

"Oh?" I ask.

"Yeah, among the three of us, Asher has always been the most … straightlaced, let's say."

I raise my eyebrows. "And you aren't?"

Aiden levels me with a look. "Do I seem straightlaced to you?"

I laugh out loud at this. "No," I admit. "You do not."

I stare down at the cocktail in my hands as a silence settles around us. I'm suddenly hyper aware of how close Aiden is to me, his leg barely touching mine, the heat from his body on my skin.

"Did I tell you how beautiful you look in this?" Aiden says softly, reaching over to my knee to gently brush his fingers against the fabric of my dress.

My heart rate speeds up, my breath somehow shallow and fast. I turn my head to find him already staring at me. "I know what you're trying to do," I breathe.

His lip twitches upward in a smile. "Oh yeah? And what am I trying to do?"

I swallow. "Compliment me, flatter me."

He raises an eyebrow. "And what's so bad about that?"

He's inching closer to me, his face barely a foot from mine.

"Because you're the type of man used to getting whatever he wants. And you can't have me." I say it slowly, with a smirk of my own. But I'm afraid my tone, my body language, my eyes, are giving me away.

Betraying what I really feel. *You can't have me*. Little does he know he already does.

Or maybe he knows exactly what I'm trying so desperately to hide.

A spark of delight flashes across his face, and he leans in impossibly closer. "And what *you* do want, Lilly?" He gently reaches up to caress my cheek. My body is frozen, only aware of the place where his skin is meeting mine.

I open my mouth, but no words come out.

"I'll tell you what *I* want," he says slowly, his caress trailing gently down my neck, sending shivers across my skin. "I want to do terrible, unspeakable things to you. I want you naked underneath me while you make the most delicious noises known to man. I want you screaming my name and begging for more. But first …" He pauses. "I want to kiss you."

The silence stretches around us, enveloping us, crushing us. My body is on fire, my face red and hot, my nerves alight with electricity. I take in a shaky breath. *What are you doing, Lilly? What are you doing?* I ask myself. But it's too late. It was already too late the second I laid eyes on him. "Then do it," I find myself answering, my voice barely audible.

Before I have time to second guess my decision, Aiden's mouth is on mine, his hands on my waist, pulling me close to him. The kiss is desperate, passionate, deep, and despite my better judgement, I am utterly lost in anything and everything Aiden.

My body melts into him as he kisses me, as he wraps his arms around me and pulls me closer. He pushes me backward against the sofa, and the drink in my hand falls, clattering to the floor with a splash. I gasp in shock, starting to sit up. "Oh no, should I—"

But Aiden is pushing me back down. "Someone else can clean that up," he murmurs, pressing a kiss to the nape of my neck. My eyes flutter closed, and I find myself agreeing, melting into the couch, submitting to his touch.

His hands roam across my stomach, up and across my breasts, squeezing them gently through the satin fabric of my dress. I moan softly.

"You're not wearing a bra," he breathes, gently teasing my nipple through the thin, satin fabric.

I feel myself redden. He's right, I'm not. The dress didn't work with one. It hasn't been noticeable until now. Glancing down, I can see the outline of my taut nipples through the fabric. I look up at him, biting my lip.

"Fuck, that's hot," he murmurs, leaning down to continue kissing my neck. He softly pinches my nipple through the fabric, and a quiet yelp escapes me. I gasp as the slight pain and pleasure mix together in an unfamiliar way. I've never had a man do that to me before. I've never had a man do … well, a lot of things.

But before I have time to dwell on that, Aiden is focusing on my other nipple, teasing it alive through the fabric and making me squirm. Slowly, he slides the thin straps of my dress over my shoulders, kissing his way down my neck, my collarbone, to the tops of my breasts. Then, slowly, he slides the satin fabric down to my stomach, exposing me to the room.

I gasp as a rush of cold air glides across my breasts, hardening my nipples even more. Aiden takes a moment to gaze down at me, and I can feel myself reddening in embarrassment. Holy shit. Aiden King is staring at my bare breasts. Aiden King is … oh my god. Is he going to—?

But my train of thought is immediately stopped when he lowers his head and takes one of my nipples in his mouth. A deep moan escapes me as pleasure courses through my body. Fuck, that feels good. It feels amazing. It feels unlike anything I've ever experienced.

His tongue flicks across my nipple, back and forth, speeding up, and I cry out softly. He nibbles gently, and I grip his biceps, desperate for more. He moves to my other breast, doing the same until I'm a moaning, whimpering puddle of pleasure, completely at his mercy.

When he's done with my breasts, leaving them red and swollen, he runs a hand lazily along my thigh, snaking it under my dress and slowly reaching up, up, up. My breath hitches in my throat as he nears my center.

Sure, I've fooled around with guys before, but not like this. Not like …

Fuck, I can't tell Aiden. I can't tell him. I can't tell anyone. But can I simply go on like this?

He slips his finger into my panties, running it along my slit. He groans when he feels how wet I am, lazily drawing his finger up to my clit and rubbing.

I buck my hips, gasping at the sensation.

Aiden presses his body down on mine, kissing my neck and up to my ear. "Fuck Lilly, I love the noises you make," he whispers, his breath hot against my skin.

I whimper as he picks up speed.

God, it feels incredible. He's incredible. The only thought I can get through my fuzzy brain is the idea of

Aiden deep inside me. I've never felt like this before. Never wanted someone so badly. I'm aching for him, desperate, out of my mind.

But should I do this? Am I *about* to do this? Go farther than simply fooling around on the couch? I try to get myself to think straight, to see the situation for what it is, but Aiden's fingers are driving me wild, chasing all sensibility from my head.

Maybe now is the time. Maybe now is perfect.

Chapter 10

Aiden

Lilly's soft, desperate moans fill the room, echoing in my ears like a melody. I trail kisses down her neck, across her collarbone and then her soft, plump breasts, pink and swollen from how I'd teased them. The fabric of her blue dress is bunched around her waist, my hand up her skirt pleasuring her, her bare breasts heaving as she moans and gasps.

It's the most beautiful fucking thing I've ever seen.

My cock aches in my pants, stretching against the tight fabric, begging to be released. Fuck, all I want is to plunge deep into her soaking wet pussy, to watch the pleasure wash across her face, to make her scream.

I rub my finger faster against her clit. Her mouth opens in ecstasy, and I think she's getting close. Her nails dig into the meat on my upper arms. Her gaze meets mine, her desire echoing mine.

But I don't want her to come just yet. I want her coming around my cock, her pussy squeezing me as I empty myself inside of her. Still rubbing her clit, although slower, I lean down to brush my lips against her ear. "I have a condom in my wallet," I breathe.

A soft breath escapes her. I lean back to look in her eyes. That desire is still there, although I think I see something else too. Something I can't quite pinpoint.

I run my free hand along one of her breasts, teasing her nipple. She shudders. "I want to be inside you so badly," I whisper.

Her body tenses. At first, I think it's in reaction to what I'm doing—still rubbing her clit, her breast. She takes in a shuddering breath, and then a completely new emotion flashes across her face. Is that … fear?

She pushes against me, scrambling to sit up. I immediately relent, leaning back, alarmed. "Is everything okay?" I ask quickly.

She hurries to cover herself, pulling up her dress. "Yes, everything's—everything's okay," she stammers, looking anywhere but at me.

"What's wrong?" I ask, reaching for her, but she stands before I can touch her.

She twirls to face me, a fake smile plastered across her face. "Nothing." She's shaking her head. "Nothing. I just ... it's late, I should probably go home."

"Are you sure?" I stand as well, every nerve in my body on fire. What happened? What did I do? What did I do to cause that flash of fear I'd seen in her face? My stomach is tying itself in knots, making me practically nauseous. "Lilly, what's wrong? Did I do something?"

She continues shaking her head, taking a step back from me.

I halt, her fear, her trepidation like a dagger through my heart. Fuck. What did I do? Did I push her too far? Did I scare her? "Lilly, if I did anything, I'm so sorry," I begin.

"You didn't—you didn't do anything wrong," she cuts me off. "I have to go, Aiden. I'm sorry. I'll see you at work on Monday."

And with that, she twirls and practically runs from the room.

I stand in silence, the crackling of the fireplace the only sound. I have the sudden urge to run after her—to chase her down, figure out what's wrong, hold her in my arms. But then I worry it could only make things worse. Scare her, even?

A pit grows in my stomach at the thought of having made Lilly react that way. I rerun everything in my mind. I run my fingers through my hair and sit back down on the couch, holding my head in my hands. Because, to my surprise, a realize a new motivation is beginning to sprout. Sure, I'd wanted to sleep with Lilly since the moment I saw her. She's gorgeous and stunning. But not only that. She's sweet and smart, and I love the sound of her laugh. She makes me smile just by walking into a room.

I don't just want to sleep with Lilly, I want …

Fuck, what do I want? I don't know. The only thing I'm certain of right now is that I have to fix whatever I did. Whatever I did to make her feel the way she did, to make her run out of here as if the room was on fire, I have to fix it.

Chapter 11

Lilly

I sit in the empty classroom at the back of the building, my laptop open on the table in front of me. I glance at the clock on the wall. It's almost three.

I sigh, leaning back in my chair and rubbing my temples.

I've been avoiding Aiden all day. I knew he was here when I'd first shown up to work. That black Porche in the parking lot certainly doesn't belong to anyone else. He'd noticed me walking by his office and had started to stand, but I'd rushed away before he had a chance to say anything.

And now I've been here all day. In the one classroom that doesn't have a class being taught in it.

So far, no one's come to bother me. I'm hoping Aiden isn't determined enough to search the entire building for me.

Part of me feels guilty for how I'd run away from the wedding on Saturday. I knew it was childish, embarrassing. That I should have at least spoken to him, but I could barely think straight. The only thing running through my mind was pure humiliation. Humiliation at having to tell Aiden why I'd completely freaked out.

Of course I'd enjoyed what we'd been doing. I'd loved every second of it. The way his hands roamed my body, made me gasp. The things he'd whispered in my ear. My core warms now just thinking about it.

And the further we went, the more and more I wanted him. I wanted him desperately, more than I've ever wanted anyone. But …

I couldn't stand the thought of telling him the one thing I've been so ashamed of my entire adult life.

The thing other men have pressed for but never got from me.

Sex.

My face warms in frustration, the familiar embarrassment and shame flooding back to me. At twenty-four, I'm well beyond my years in many things. I have an established career, I'm good with money, I've traveled the world.

And yet, I'm so, so woefully behind when it comes to the one thing that everyone seems to care about.

And to be honest, there's really no reason for it. It's not like I'm saving myself for marriage or have some hangup about sex. I haven't had sex yet simply because I haven't met someone I was willing to give it up for. It's as simple as that.

I always thought I'd fall in love and sex would happen naturally. And then as the years went on and it never happened, suddenly a random hookup was no longer an acceptable way to lose one's virginity. What was I supposed to do? Casually suggest my first time happens after a Tinder date? Maybe I could have gotten away with something like that in college, but not now. Not in my twenties.

And so here I am, twenty-four and a virgin.

I glare angrily out the window. Angry at myself for freaking out this weekend and running away from the first man in forever who I've had any kind of spark with. Angry at myself for not just going for it, for letting it happen. Angry at myself for letting myself stay a virgin this long.

Overwhelmed, I bury my head in my hands and groan.

"Rough day?" a voice calls, and I straighten. "I was wondering where you were," Monica says, walking into the room.

I chuckle, somewhat embarrassed. "Yeah, I'm … hiding from Aiden," I admit.

She raises her eyebrows. "Why?"

"We went to his brother's wedding on Saturday."

Her eyes widen like saucers. "What?" She hurries across the room, pulling up a chair beside me. "You went to Asher King's wedding with Aiden?"

I nod.

Monica makes an expression that can only be described as pure glee. "Oh my god," she gushes. "Tell me everything."

I tell her about the wedding, how beautiful it was, how Aiden and I had danced, and then how things had become heated. "The only problem is … I kind ran away at the last minute."

Monica frowns in confusion. "Ran away?" she echoes.

I purse my lips, nodding. Like most people in my life, Monica isn't privy to the details of my sex life, so I hedge around the truth. "I just freaked out. I got in my head and ran away."

She nods, giving me a sympathetic look. "How do you feel now?" she asks.

I take a moment. How *do* I feel now? "I guess I'm not sure."

"Do you like him?"

"Yes." The answer comes so quickly, I barely have time to process it.

"Okay. Then talk to him."

She states it so simply, but I suppose she's right. I should just talk to him. At the very least, I think he's owed an explanation. It's probably a bit unfair that I've spent the day avoiding him.

After a few more minutes of talk, Monica heads off, and I go back to work. I contemplate moving back to my office, but the nerves dancing in my lower belly stop me. The idea of seeing Aiden, of facing him after my embarrassing actions, is overwhelming. I wonder if I can get away with just one more day. One more night to think about it, and then I can talk to him in the morning.

I finish up the rest of my work and head back to my office just a bit after five. Aiden should be gone by now—everyone should be gone by now.

I walk down the quiet, empty corridors, glancing into Aiden's office as I pass it. I was right; he's gone. A mixture of relief and disappointment flash through me, but I push both of those emotions away as I enter my office.

When I notice a figure sitting at my desk, I jump, a small shriek of surprise escaping my lip.

Aiden looks up, alarmed. "Lilly," he says quickly, standing. "I wanted to talk."

I compose myself, trying to put a mask of nonchalance over my expression. "Hi," I say softly.

"I wanted to apologize about the wedding," Aiden says quickly, his eyebrows furrowed together in distress. "If I did anything that made you uncomfortable—"

"No, Aiden, you didn't," I interrupt him. "*I'm* sorry. I should have—I shouldn't have just run off like that."

"I was worried I'd scared you, that I'd pushed you too far or something," Aiden continues.

I'm shaking my head. "It's not that at all."

"I shouldn't have moved things so quickly," he goes on. "I should have paid more attention to you, to the situation—"

"I'm a virgin," I suddenly blurt out.

He stops short, his gaze meeting mine from across the room. Confusion washes over his face, then shock. He opens his mouth, but no words come out.

"I was ... *very* into what was happening," I admit, feeling myself reddening. "I'm into *you*. But ... I didn't want to ruin the mood by telling you I'd never had sex before, but I couldn't just go through with it, and I—I freaked out." I hadn't really expected to be this honest, but here we are. I bite my lip, feeling the embarrassment rushing through me. I've just told him my most intimate secret, and there's no going back.

The silence stretches around us, suffocating me. *God, say something. Say anything*, I plead. But as the seconds tick by, I can't take it any longer.

I sling my purse over my shoulder, head down, and rush toward the door. "I shouldn't have told you. I should've known it would be too much," I mutter.

But before I can exit, Aiden rushes across the room and blocks me, closing the door with a click. I look up, his arm extended, leaning against the door, his frame towering over me. "You think I care that you're a virgin?" he asks slowly, a frown crinkling across his face. "You think that's too much for me?" He raises an eyebrow.

"I ..." I stutter. "Sometimes it is for people," I admit.

Surprise flashes across his face, and then there's that smile again—that slight smirk that lights my lower belly on fire. "If you think I'm going to be scared off that easily, you're wrong."

I smile softly at this, a strange mixture of relief and arousal coursing through me. "Yeah?" I ask.

"You called it at the wedding," he says, his voice low as he leans closer to me. "I'm a man who's used to getting what he wants. And want *you*. I don't care about the incidentals."

My breath catches in my throat.

Aiden reaches for me, tucking a stand of hair behind my ear. "How about I take you on a real date?" he says.

Chapter 12

Aiden

Lilly sits in the passenger seat of my Porsche as I drive us to the restaurant. I'd chosen one of my favorites off the top of my head. An upscale Italian place slightly more downtown than the foundation, but definitely worth the drive. It's a Monday night, so I'm hoping we'll be okay to show up without a reservation. And if not, I have my ways of getting a table.

I keep glancing at her out of the corner of my eye. Her hair is pulled back into a low, messy bun, and she's clutching her purse in her lap somewhat nervously. She's seemed a little on edge ever since her admission a few minutes ago. Is it embarrassment, maybe?

I'd tried to keep the shock off my face when she'd told me she was a virgin. I'm still trying to keep the shock at bay now. But holy shit. A virgin?

How does a girl who looks like that end up a virgin at twenty-four? Surely she's had dozens of men lining up, desperate for any crumb she'd throw them. It definitely can't be from lack of male interest. Is she one of those religious types? I doubt so, considering she's never mentioned it.

A small string of guilt gnaws at my insides remembering the wedding last weekend. It makes sense now why she'd run off. Why she'd gotten nervous and overwhelmed. I wish she'd just told me then. I would have slowed things way down, let her take the lead.

Speaking of which, I realize that things with Lilly will have to go slowly from here. And to my utter shock, I'm totally okay with it. More than okay with it. I'm determined to get to know her, learn more about her, inside and out. Normally, a girl who required this much effort … well, I'd have moved on by now. But there's something about Lilly that's different. Something about her that gets me thinking about more than just sleeping with her. Yeah, of course, that would be great, but I find myself daydreaming about other things. Simply spending time with her. Laughing. Hanging out.

I almost laugh out loud at the absurdity. Aiden from a month ago would be appalled. Never did he think a girl would be worth the effort.

Boy was he wrong.

When we walk into the restaurant, Lilly's eyes widen in awe at the grandeur of the place. She looks around, taking it all in. The chandeliers hanging from the ceiling, the elegant décor, the chinking of wine glasses.

"This place looks … *nice*," she comments quietly.

"It is," I say with a shrug.

We're shown to a table, and we take our seats. Lilly glances around the room, seemingly avoiding eye contact. There's an awkwardness in the air between us, something I'm hoping will dissipate with some wine and conversation. I don't want her to feel awkward, embarrassed. I want her to feel like we did at the wedding. Carefree, happy. I shoot her a warm smile, and she sends a hesitant one back to me.

The waiter comes for our drink order, and we each choose a glass of wine.

"How is yours?" I ask gently after she takes her first sip.

"Good." She smiles.

After a pause, I say, "I meant what I said at the wedding."

She looks at me quizzically. "What did you say?"

"About being interested in your ideas for the foundation," I remind her with a smile.

Some of the tension eases, and she smiles back at me. "Really?" She raises an eyebrow. "You aren't just saying that?"

I shoot her a look. "You think I got where I am today by giving people false praise?"

She laughs.

The waiter politely interrupts our conversation to take our meal orders and then disappears.

"I like your idea about an art show," I continue. "Tell me more about that."

She seems slightly hesitant, like she still thinks I'm only feigning interest to be polite, but she answers anyway. "I think it could be an excellent way to raise money for the foundation. And that's what you guys are worried about, right? The funds?"

I shrug. "It's a minor concern. Mainly we want to make sure the money is being well spent and that it's not a *waste* of money. But fundraising is something the foundation seems to be struggling with, from the records I've seen."

"We are," Lilly admits. "The things we're doing now just aren't working. And the kids we help don't come from families who can give donations or anything like that—which we don't expect at all, but obviously that makes it hard to run the foundation."

I nod.

"But think about how cool an art show could be." Her eyes light up a bit at this, and she leans forward, propping her elbows on the table. "We could display art the kids have created, or maybe showcase a specific artist—like the high school kids we award scholarships to every year. We could auction off a few pieces, have wine and food provided, turn it into a whole event that people can buy tickets for."

I'm nodding along, listening more closely than I had at the wedding. Just like I'd thought last time, this *is* a pretty good idea. "And you mentioned that my brothers and I could dip into our more affluent list of contacts for attendance," I remind her.

She grins, shrugging. "Why not? It's your mother's foundation, after all. It's meaningful. And isn't that what rich socialites love? Attending meaningful events?"

I smirk. "I suppose you're right."

"I'm always right," she says playfully, taking a sip of her wine.

I chuckle. "I'll try to remember that."

Our food arrives shortly, and we dig in. After a few bites, I say, "I really like this idea, Lilly. I really do."

She meets my gaze, hesitant hope in her eyes.

"Let's make this happen. You and me."

Chapter 13

Lilly

When we finish dinner, we get into Aiden's car, heading back toward the foundation. But when Aiden pulls out into the road, traffic eastward looks like a nightmare. A line of red taillights shows cars backed up for seemingly miles.

He huffs in mild frustration. "Traffic here is so unpredictable."

I nod, staring out the window. "You know, my place isn't far from here. You could just drop me off at home, and I can get an Uber to work in the morning," I suggest.

He glances over at me. "You sure?"

I nod.

He manages to pull off onto a side road and turn around, and I tell him which direction to head in.

"And don't worry about calling your own Uber in the morning, I'll set one up for you," he says offhandedly.

I chuckle in surprise. "You don't have to do that," I protest.

He holds up a hand. "I took you on a date and wasn't able to get you back to your car. *I'll* call your Uber in the morning." He says it in a way that assertively ends the conversation.

"Thank you," I finally say with a soft smile.

I continue to give Aiden directions as we near my apartment. When he finally pulls into the complex parking lot, he parks in front of my building.

"I'll walk you to your door," he says, hopping out of the car.

I shoot him a shy smile as we make our way up the steps to my apartment door. We stand awkwardly for a few heartbeats, neither of us seemingly wanting to say goodbye. I glance at the time on my phone. It isn't all that late. And I've had a wonderful time with him so far. Would it be weird to invite him inside?

"Do you want to see my apartment?" I finally blurt out.

He smiles. "See where Lilly Richards spends her evenings? I'd love to."

I laugh, unlocking my door and stepping over the threshold. I flip the lights on, stepping aside so Aiden can enter and then closing the door behind him.

He walks farther in, looking around. The apartment is small. The main room constitutes as a living room and kitchen space with nice, large windows over the couch on the far wall. My bedroom and bathroom are off to the right through two doors.

Aiden quickly zeroes in on a painting on the wall. He approaches it, glancing over his shoulder at me.

"You did this." It isn't really a question, more of a statement.

"How'd you know?" I laugh.

"It's like your other ones at the foundation," he says, turning back to it. "You use similar colors. Similar ... ways of expressing things."

I walk up beside him, looking at the painting as well. "I did it in college. It's of the fields by my parents' house where I grew up."

Aiden cocks his head. "It's beautiful."

I can feel myself blushing, and I hope he doesn't notice. "Thank you."

We stand like that, side by side, our arms barely touching, for a few heavy minutes, silence hanging around us. I keep glancing sideways at him. At the sharp edges of his jawline, the five o'clock shadow on his skin, at his hands in the pockets of his dress pants.

I feel that familiar longing I'd felt at the wedding. The desire for his hands to be all over me. To do what they'd done only a few nights ago.

Aiden turns to me as if feeling the air change between us. His eyes search mine—for what, I don't know. Is he thinking the same thing I am? And as the tension between us grows—torn between right and wrong, desire and need—I do the only thing I can think of.

I span the distance between us, grab the collar of his shirt, and I kiss him.

He freezes, and for a split second I think I've made a terrible mistake. That I've misread the situation. That I've ruined everything.

But then his hands grip my upper arms, and he kisses me back. Hard. Desperate. As if he's suffocating and I'm the only air in the room.

We stumble backward, nearly tripping over each other until my back hits the wall. I throw my arms around his neck, pulling him closer to me. His tongue swirls against mine as our kiss deepens.

His hands roam up, over my shoulders, my neck, and into my hair. His touch is gentle, sweet.

I breathe in the scent of him—cologne, sweat, and purely *Aiden*.

Then he pulls back, his gaze meeting mine, our faces inches apart, breathing heavily. There's a question in those deep blue eyes.

"Lilly," he breathes. "I want to make sure you're okay with everything."

I nod, staring up at him. "I'm ... not ready for sex, but—I had to kiss you," I whisper.

He nods. "We won't do anything until you want to," he declares. "What we did at the wedding—were you okay with that?" He searches my gaze genuinely.

I nod. I was.

He smiles, leaning down to plant a soft kiss right below my ear. "Let me make you feel good, Lilly," he whispers, his breath hot against my neck.

I sigh.

"Can I make you feel good?" he asks.

"Yes," I breathe.

Still pressing kisses down my neck, he reaches up to gently unbutton my blouse. In a few moments, he's sliding it off my shoulders, revealing a pink bralette. His hands skim up my arms, across my shoulders, stopping at the strap of my bra. He seems hesitant. Worried, almost. As if afraid he might break me.

I look up at him. "Touch me," I whisper.

His breath hitches in his throat, his eyes alight with desire. He slowly slides the strap of my bra off my shoulder, then reaches around to unclasp it in the back. It falls to the floor.

His hands slide across my arms to cup my breasts, and I sigh.

"Fuck," Aiden whispers, looking down at me.

He draws a soft finger down my neck and chest, then over my breasts, making low circles on each one, ending with a soft pinch of my nipples.

I gasp quietly at the sensation. He leans down, his breath hot against my chest, taking a nipple into his mouth and running his tongue softly over the bud. I arch my back into him, squeezing my eyes shut in pleasure. His hand finds my other breast, massaging it gently.

Fuck, I'm so wet. I'm imagining him plunging deep inside of me, filling my aching pussy. I want him so badly. I've never wanted someone so badly. I actually want Aiden to fuck me.

He continues to flick my nipple with his tongue, causing me to moan and writhe in pleasure. It's almost torture.

He lifts his head and shoots me a devilish smile. I'm panting from the sensations, my chest rising and falling, my nipples hardened into tight, erect buds.

I reach up to grasp the back of his neck and pull him down into a kiss. He devours me, kneading my breasts as he kisses me deeply. I moan into his mouth.

Suddenly, he hooks his hands under my thighs, hoisting me up, my legs wrapped around his waist. I squeal in surprise as he carries me over to the couch, depositing me gently onto it and crawling over top of me.

Aiden trails kisses up my bare stomach, across my breasts, and to my neck.

I dig my nails into his back, pulling him closer. His lips pressed against my ear, he murmurs, "I want to taste you, Lilly." He leans back just enough to meet my gaze. "But only if you want me to."

My breath hitches in my throat, nerves dancing in my belly. While everything we've done so far isn't completely new to me, and I've had guys touch me pretty much everywhere, I've never actually had a man go down on me.

But I know the answer before I even have to think about it. And my body is giving me away. I nod. "I want you to," I admit.

His eyes light up, and he slides down the couch, kneeling on the end of it as he reaches for my jeans, slowly unbuttoning them. He slides them off effortlessly, leaving me in nothing but a pair of white panties. He hooks a finger under the band, sending one last questioning glance up at me before slowly pulling them down my legs.

And there I am, completely and utterly naked in front of Aiden King. He spends a moment taking me in, devouring every inch of me with his eyes.

He runs a hand up my thigh, squeezing gently. "Fuck," he murmurs. "You're perfect."

I feel myself reddening—both at his compliment and his perusal.

He leans down to press a soft kiss to my bare stomach, kissing lower and lower. Then he parts my legs, settling between them and kissing from my knee up my inner thigh. My breath quickens in anticipation. I can barely believe what's happening. Aiden King is between my legs.

A quick jolt of self-consciousness shoots through me. I've exposed my most intimate part of my body to him, and his face is barely inches away from it. But as he continues to kiss and caress my flesh, I find myself melting into the couch cushions below me.

He looks up, and his gaze meets mine as he lowers his face, pressing a soft kiss to my center. Then he licks slowly along my slit.

My mouth opens in a shocked and pleasured gasp.

He reaches my clit, slowly flicking his tongue back and forth across my bud. I grit my teeth, holding back a cry.

He speeds up, his fingers digging into the flesh of my thighs, holding me open. I pant in desperation, bucking my hips.

I reach down to grasp his hair, running my fingers along his scalp.

He sucks gently on my bud, and I cry out in ecstasy. "Oh god," I whine, my fingers leaving Aiden's hair to grip the couch cushions beneath me. "*Aiden,*" I breathe.

He raises his head, his finger immediately taking the spot his tongue had been occupying. "Do you feel good, Lilly?" he asks.

I nod desperately, the pleasure building inside of me.

Aiden reaches up with his free hand to caress one of my heaving breasts, teasing my nipple. I bite my lip, moaning.

"I wanna make you come so bad," he murmurs, his gaze trailing my naked body. "Are you gonna come for me?"

"I—I think so," I stutter.

"Good."

He lowers his head back to my center, his tongue continuing to flick my bud over and over again. A strangled cry of pleasure escapes me—sounds I never knew I was even capable of making. In an ordinary situation, I'd be embarrassed, I'd be mortified at my naked body, these ridiculous noises, the fact that I'm letting Aiden King do what he's doing to me.

But all I can think about right now is the pleasure he's putting me through.

I'm panting, crying out desperately. I feel the pleasure building and building. And finally, my orgasm crashes through me. I cry out, my legs shaking as wave after wave of my climax rushes through me.

Aiden leans back with a satisfied grin, watching me writhe and shake in ecstasy. He leans down to press a soft kiss to my cheek. "Good girl," he whispers.

Chapter 14

Lilly

True to his word, Aiden sends an Uber to pick me up in the morning. I walk past my parked car in the parking lot, noticing that Aiden isn't here yet, and make my way to my office.

I sit down, opening my laptop. I still can't believe what happened last night. My brain is still fuzzy and giddy, overwhelmed.

I went on a date with Aiden King. Aiden King. The man I thought was going to be the end of my job. The man I was thoroughly irritated by for a good week or so. The man I found myself frustratingly, overwhelmingly attracted to.

And then he'd taken me home, spread me out on my couch, and pleasured me until I'd seen stars. My pulse speeds up just thinking about it.

I close my eyes, taking a deep breath. Oh my god. I can't even believe the things he'd made me feel. I think back to his snide comments when we'd first met—about how he knew how to make a girl feel good in the bedroom. I have to admit he wasn't lying.

And what's more amazing was his reaction to my secret. The secret I've kept from so many people. The secret that's ended many previous relationships. The thing I've come to be so ashamed of. My virginity.

I was so certain he'd run. Many men have. But especially Aiden King. He could have any girl he wants. He could sleep with any girl he wants, no playing hard to get, no strings attached. Why would he want to deal with me? A girl who's never had sex before? I'm more hassle than it's worth.

But apparently, Aiden disagrees.

I hear footsteps down the hall and look up to see Aiden entering his office. He glances through the window of my office door, and when our eyes meet, he smiles.

Butterflies pool in my stomach.

Shit. I'm really in trouble now, aren't I? But I can't stop the stupid grin from spreading across my face.

Aiden enters my office, that familiar smirk warming my belly. "Hey," he says, his voice soft.

"Hey yourself," I greet him.

"I thought if you didn't have anything more pressing today, we could go over that art show idea. Make some actual plans," he suggests.

My eyes widen in pleasant surprise. Even though we've talked about the idea a few times, I'm still shocked that he's actually wanting to go through with it. Pour hours and time and money into it.

I nod. "Yes. That'd be great."

"Mind if I join you in here?"

My smile widens. "Go for it."

The hours pass easily as Aiden and I go over more ideas for the Maria King Foundation art show. He pulls out lists of names to invite, event companies to hire, and I go over art show protocol, speeches, and auction etiquette. We choose a date at the end of the month. I worry it's too soon, but Aiden assures me he can rally up enough attendees. Besides, he reminds me, the foundation's art shows are going to be a regular installation. A new part of the fabric of King Tech and the Maria King Foundation.

"What about the actual art?" Aiden asks at one point.

I nod, thinking. "There are lots of options. We could find a local artist willing to donate some of their work. Or we could showcase some of the students' art."

"This first show has to be good," Aiden presses. "It has to be really impressive."

I find myself laughing. "You don't believe in the students here?"

He snorts. "I'm sorry, it's not that. It's just … I really want this to succeed." He pauses for a moment, looking at me. "I want *you* to succeed."

Slightly taken aback at the sincerity of his statement, I look away, smiling. "It'll succeed," I assure him. "Don't worry."

Chapter 15

Aiden

As the day draws to a close, I glance up at Lilly from across the desk. Last night had been incredible. I'd spent the rest of the evening imagining her naked body, the sounds she'd made, and jerking myself off to it in the shower. I hadn't asked for any return of the favor. In fact, when she'd asked if I wanted her to, I'd simply shaken my head. She'd looked so confused, so shocked. It almost made me laugh.

But I hadn't wanted her to feel uncomfortable, out of place. All I'd wanted to do was pleasure her. To focus on *her*. And that's exactly what I did.

And spending all day with her today—going over work stuff, at that—has been so ... easy. Like breathing. I find myself laughing over the stupidest things. Things that don't matter. Things that are just silly.

I see Lilly glancing at the time on her phone. It's definitely past 5 at this point.

"We should probably call it a day," she says, glancing up at me.

"Come to my place," I say without thinking. I don't know what's come over me, but I'm desperate to see more of her, to spend as much time with her as possible. I've never felt this way about a woman before. Not like this. "We can have dinner and wine."

Her eyes widen in surprise, but then she smiles, to my relief. "I suppose I could be convinced," she says coyly.

I chuckle. "Oh, I'll convince you."

Delighted surprise flashes across her face before she stands, gathering her coat and purse. "Okay, Casanova," she says with a laugh. "Lead the way."

I insist upon a driving, and her slight protests are met with, "I'll call you an Uber home and another one to work in the morning."

"You own stock in that company or something?" she asks with a smirk, settling into the passenger seat of my Porsche. I chuckle.

The drive to my place isn't long. I live downtown—technically the same building as Asher and Alec. We'd all bought penthouse suites in the same complex. It was one of our first big purchases together once the company took off. We'd toured places together and when we'd happened upon a building with three penthouses available at the same time, we'd thought it was fate or something like that. Or at least an opportunity too good to pass up.

I pull into the garage, park the car, and we head toward the main doors. When we enter the lobby, I can see Lilly's eyes go wide.

We ride up the elevator, and after I punch in a keycode, we step into a lavishly decorated lobby. My unit is to the right, so I open the door and step inside, holding the door for Lilly.

Her mouth drops open when she takes in the sight of my apartment. I'll admit it—it's pretty nice. Floor-to-ceiling windows cover the entire living area, showing off a beautiful view of downtown Seattle. I can even see the Space Needle from here.

I had an interior designer put together my furniture and décor, so it definitely feels homey and aesthetically pleasing, although I never could have come up with it on my own.

Lilly quickly shuts her mouth, turning to me and smiling softly. "This is place is … very nice," she says.

I laugh. "You can say it. It's a little over the top, I know."

She laughs too. "I'm just surprised. I suppose I shouldn't be, though. You are, after all, Aiden King."

I purse my lips. "That's me."

I'd ordered takeout before we left the foundation, but the restaurant I'd ordered from is notorious for being busy. It probably won't be ready for a little while.

"Wine?" I offer, striding to the kitchen and pulling two wine glasses from a cabinet.

"Yes, thank you," Lilly says.

"Red or white?" I ask.

She purses her lips in thought. "White," she decides.

I pour two glasses and lead the way into the living room, settling in on the couch. Lilly takes a seat beside me, and I hand her a glass.

She takes a sip. I find myself unable to stop glancing at her. At the way her hair frames her face, the way her nose crinkles when she smiles.

"Your art," I finally ask. "Were you always a painter?"

She twirls the wine gently in her glass. "Pretty much. I played with colored pencils as a kid, and as soon as my parents trusted me with paints, I'd spend pretty much every afternoon doing just that."

I nod. "Well, it shows."

She shoots me a shy look and then shrugs. "It's just for fun."

It's my turn to shoot her a look. "It doesn't have to be just for fun," I press. "You're good enough to be an actual artist. To get paid for it. Recognized."

She shakes her head. "No. But that's okay, really. I'm happy just doing it."

I want to press her on it, make her realize how good her stuff really is, but I drop it for the moment.

"How about your mom?" Lilly asks. "I know the foundation was named after her and that she enjoyed the arts. Was she an artist too?"

The memory of Mom settles over me. While it used to make me sad, it's simply bittersweet now. I nod. "She painted too. Well, she did just about everything." I laugh. "Painting, sculpting, knitting—if it was artistic, she did it."

Lilly smiles.

I stare down at my wine. "She'd be happy to know the foundation is doing good."

Lilly's expression softens. "So you *do* think it's doing good? You believe that? After all your research through our expenses and files?" She chuckles softly, but I can tell it's a genuine inquiry.

"I do," I admit honestly. "The testimonies from college kids we've given scholarships to. The community it's created for kids and families."

Lilly smirks. "You said you only cared about the financial records."

I roll my eyes. "I *do* care about the financial records. Doesn't mean I didn't look through the file you emailed me labeled *Student Success Stories*."

Lilly laughs, setting her drink down on the coffee table. "I suppose that was a bit heavy handed."

I shrug. "It got the job done."

"And what about you?" Lilly asks. "Any artistic tendencies get transferred to you?"

I snort. "Not an iota. I'm all math and business. I suppose that's part of why King Tech got to where it is."

Lilly cocks her head. "You're probably right." She tucks her knees up under her, leaning over and snuggling against me. Butterflies clamor in my stomach, and I reach my arm around her, tucking her closer to me.

I gaze down at the top of her head, reaching up to gently run my fingers through her golden hair. We stay like that for a few moments, Lilly leaning against me while I play with her hair.

After a while, she angles her head up to meet my gaze, and I see something in her eyes. Something I can't quite identify. Nerves? Excitement? Both?

"You know," she says softly. "You didn't let me return the favor last night."

I'm momentarily puzzled until the realization settles over me. What we'd done last night. Or really, what *I'd* done. I smile. "I didn't want you to feel pressured," I admit. And I still don't.

"That's it?" she presses.

I raise an eyebrow at her. "You don't think I wouldn't have liked it, do you?" I laugh.

She giggles, and just then I notice her hand moving along my thigh. "So you *would* like it?" she asks, somewhat hesitantly.

Hyperaware of her hand inching closer and closer to my crotch, my breath hitches in my throat. I meet her gaze. "Only if you want to," I say, trying to keep my voice firm. "And I mean it—only if you want to."

"I do want to," she breathes.

My cock pulses at her response. Fuck. The idea of her mouth wrapped around my cock sends hot waves of arousal through me. It's doing things that no other fantasy ever has. "Have you ever …?"

She pauses for a moment and then shakes her head, suddenly looking worried, embarrassed. And all I want to do is wipe that embarrassment away, make her feel desired, beautiful, confident. I reach out to run my thumb along her cheek. "You don't have to unless you want to," I say again, worried that maybe her hesitancy isn't just from nerves.

But she allays those fears with a shake of her head. "I want to, Aiden. Believe me." With that, she slides off the couch, positioning herself between my knees.

I unbuckle my belt and unzip my pants, freeing my cock. It's already partially hard, and Lilly stares at it for a moment, taking it in. She seems nervous, self-conscious. She looks up to meet my gaze before reaching out to grasp the base of my cock in her small hand and guiding her mouth to it.

Starting at the base of my cock, just above my balls, she takes a long, slow lick all the way to the tip.

I sigh, my cock hardening even more.

She licks her way to the base and then to the tip again. And then, her eyes still glued to mine, she opens her mouth and slides my cock inside.

"*Fuck*," I breathe, reaching out to grasp the couch cushion beside me.

Lilly slowly starts sliding her mouth along my cock, in and out, in and out, her tongue twirling the tip. A deep groan escapes me. She'd claimed to have never done this before, but for a girl so experienced, she sure as fuck knows what to do.

She picks up speed a bit, and my cock twitches, pleasure coursing through me. Moaning softly, I take in the sight of her—Lilly on her knees between my legs, her lips stretched around my thick cock as she takes it deep into her throat.

What a good girl.

I throw my head back, closing my eyes. "Oh god, Lilly, yes," I groan.

She moans softly in response, her sounds muffled.

I can feel my climax building. I open my eyes, wanting to see Lilly—to take in the sight of her. I reach down to gently grasp a fistful of her hair in my hand.

"That's a good girl," I praise, my face contorting in ecstasy. She moans around my cock, picking up speed, saliva dripping down her chin.

A deep moan escapes me as my climax hits, my liquid spilling out of me. Lilly sputters in surprise, my cum spraying across her chin and down the front of her.

I sit up in shock, taking in the sight of her. Fuck. I should have warned her. She'd said she'd never done this. Most girls I've been with just swallow it. Or, if they want to be cummed on, they ask for it. I don't usually do it by surprise.

"I—I'm sorry," Lilly says quickly. "I wasn't really expecting …" And suddenly she bursts into laughter.

The shock slowly evaporating, I laugh too.

"I don't know what I was expecting," she says, her laughter growing more contagious. Her giggles fill the room, causing me to join in with her.

Still laughing, I lean down to take her face in both of my hands, pressing a kiss to her forehead. "I'll get you a t-shirt," I say.

Chapter 16

Lilly

Standing in Aiden's bathroom, I look at myself in the mirror. The t-shirt he'd given me hangs halfway down my bare thighs.

My discarded clothing lays in a pile on the floor. I'd been so nervous to go down on him. While I've done other stuff with guys, giving a blowjob isn't one of them. But by the way he'd reacted, he seemed to have enjoyed it. At least I hope so. Doubt and self-consciousness are beginning to creep in, but I try to push it away.

What's happening with Aiden is wholly unexpected and exciting and ... wonderful. I don't want to ruin it with my overthinking.

Taking one last glance at myself in the mirror, I leave the bathroom, stepping back out into the living room. I still can't get over the grandeur of this place. The sheer size of it—for an apartment in downtown Seattle—is absolutely insane. I suppose he is Aiden King, though.

Aiden is sitting on the couch and immediately turns his head when he hears me enter. His gaze slides along my body, lingering on my bare thighs, a soft smile on his lips.

He stands, approaching me.

I smile shyly, smoothing the t-shirt out over my hips.

Aiden reaches me, sliding his hands along my waist, gazing down at the outline of my hips. "Fuck, you look good in my t-shirt," he murmurs.

I giggle.

Aiden's hands squeeze my waist gently, then they find their way underneath the t-shirt I'm wearing, brushing against my bare skin. I suck in a soft breath. His hands travel upward, skimming over my bra.

He chuckles. "Why are you still wearing this?"

I shrug with a small laugh.

His hands snake around to my back where he deftly unclasps my bra. With some help from me, he slips the straps down my shoulders, pulling the bra out through one of the large sleeves of the t-shirt.

His hands immediately go to my breasts underneath the shirt, his thumbs gently toying with my nipples. I open my mouth, taking in a shuttering breath.

Aiden lowers his lips to my ear. "You didn't think that after what you just did to me on the couch that I wouldn't be turning you into a whimpering, moaning, little puddle, did you?"

A soft breath escapes me in response.

Suddenly, Aiden bends down to hook an arm under my knees and back, lifting me into the air. He strides across the room and through a doorway, flipping on the light switch as he enters.

The room is obviously his bedroom. A large, king-size bed sits in the center of it, complete with a matching dark blue comforter and pillow set. So coordinated for a single man. The light overhead is warm, not like those horrible fluorescents you find in most apartment buildings.

I expect him to throw me down on the bed, but instead he simply sits on the edge of it, setting me down so I'm standing in front of him, and then he spins me around, depositing my ass right on his lap.

He spreads his legs, then reaches down to grab my thigh. "Take your underwear off," he says softly.

Without thinking, I do as he says, reaching under the t-shirt to grab the hem of my panties and slide them down my legs. I toss them gently with my foot, and they land a few feet away. Aiden presses a kiss to my neck, gripping my thigh with his hand and squeezing. "Throw your legs over mine," he instructs, and with his help, I do as he says.

It's then that I see the mirror right across from us. A full-length mirror—the kind you check your outfit in before heading out for the day. Only instead, I'm faced with a vision of my legs spread over Aiden's lap, his t-shirt hiked up to my stomach, my pussy on full display.

I can't help but gasp at the sight of me. At how utterly dirty this feels. Dirty but *delicious*. Aiden rests his head against mine, meeting my gaze in the mirror. There's that smirk again. That devilishly handsome smirk that's made me tumble down a hole I'm afraid I'll never get out of.

"See how pretty you are, Lilly?" he whispers in my ear, gently running a finger up the inside of my thigh.

My mouth parts, my eyes glued to the reflection of his hand in the mirror, slowly nearing my center. My body is alight with electricity, every nerve on fire. And as I watch what Aiden is doing in the mirror, I know that he's watching what I'm doing too. How my body shakes in anticipation, how my legs are spread wide and eager for him, my center on complete and full display. *Pretty*, he'd called it.

Aiden's other hand reaches around me to grasp one of my breasts through the fabric of the t-shirt. He gently massages my nipple, causing me to moan softly.

"That's it," he murmurs, his breath warm against my ear.

His finger continues moving slowly toward my center—agonizingly so. I can see how wet I am in the reflection of the mirror. I'd be embarrassed if I weren't so desperate for him to touch me. Touch me anywhere, everywhere. Do *everything* to me.

Aiden slides a slow finger along my slit, and when he reaches my sensitive bud, I gasp in pleasure. He presses soft kisses along my neck, kisses that slowly turn into little nibbles.

He starts rubbing my clit, drawing slow circles and eliciting deep moans from within me. I buck my hips involuntarily, and he roughly squeezes my breast in response, pinching my nipple.

His finger leaves my clit, traveling down along my slit again. When his finger stops right at my opening, my breath catches in my throat.

"Lilly," Aiden whispers, and I already know what he's going to ask. And I know what my answer is. "I want my finger inside of you."

I nod, even though my body is betraying my every desire anyway. My hips are arching toward his hand, desperate. "Yes," I breathe. "Please."

Aiden grins, meeting my gaze in the mirror. "Please?" he repeats, raising an eyebrow in amusement. "You really want it bad, huh?"

I bite my lip and whimper softly in response.

His gaze darkens in desire, and his finger presses gently against my opening. Then, slowly, he slips inside of me. I gasp in pleasure, arching my back.

"Yeah?" he prompts, slowly pumping his finger in and out of me. "You like that?"

"Yes," I breathe, closing my eyes and leaning my head back against him.

He inserts his finger deep inside of me, curling it upwards as he pulls out. A blinding pleasure erupts, and a high-pitched moan fills the room.

"That's a good girl," Aiden murmurs in my ear.

I open my eyes to see my reflection in the mirror. The desperation on my face, Aiden's hand against my center. It's only now that I see he's added another finger, pumping them in and out of me, curling his fingers every time.

I open my mouth, a strangled cry escaping me. I grip Aiden's arm and his thigh beneath me, searching for anything to anchor me.

I'm panting desperately, the pleasure building and building. "Aiden," I whine.

He kisses my neck, then nibbles at my ear.

"Be my good girl and come for me," he says.

I nod.

He leans down, resting his cheek against mine. "Look at me," he orders.

I meet his gaze in the mirror, his eyes dark with desire.

"Look at me while you come," he says, his voice steady and commanding.

I nod. "Yes."

His hand that had been massaging my breast lowers, finding my clit while he continues to pump his fingers in and out of me with the other hand.

I cry out, struggling to maintain eye contact with Aiden as he'd instructed.

"Good," Aiden tells me. "That's good."

I nod, feeling myself getting closer and closer. "Oh god, Aiden," I whimper.

He nods, smiling softly at me. "Let it happen, sweetheart."

And with that, my orgasm crashes over me. I cry out, collapsing against him, my legs shaking. Aiden immediately wraps me up in his arms, pulling me against his chest as waves of my climax flow through me.

After a few moments, I finally look up at him, cradled against his chest. He grins down at me. "Stay here tonight," he whispers, and for the first time, I think I see a flash of worry in his face—as if he's afraid I might refuse.

I bite my lip. "Okay," I say, a grin spreading across my face. "I'll stay."

His smile widens, and he glances over his shoulder at the bed we're sitting on. "In case you couldn't tell, I have pretty much the nicest bed money can buy," he says. "So you're guaranteed to get the best sleep of your life." He shrugs. "Right after the best orgasm."

A shocked laugh escapes me, and I slap him playfully on the chest.

"Am I wrong?" he asks, widening his eyes at me.

I can't help it—I can feel the blush spreading across my cheeks. I look away from him, refusing to meet his eyes. "No, you're not wrong."

Chapter 17

Lilly

A soft light shines across the room, and I scrunch up my face, wondering if I'd forgotten to draw my curtains last night before going to bed. With a deep sigh, I roll over, only to remember that I'm not at home. I'm not in my bed.

I'm in Aiden King's.

He's sleeping beside me on his side, his arm thrown over my waist, his hand resting on my hip. I stare at his sleeping form, his chest rising and falling. I smile softly.

I shift again, and this time it wakes him up. He opens his eyes, and his gaze lands on mine. A smile spreads across his face.

"How'd you sleep?" he asks, his voice deep.

"Best sleep of my life."

"Told you so."

I giggle. "What time is it?"

"Doesn't matter," he responds, reaching out to wrap me in his arms and pull me against his chest.

I chuckle. "What about work?"

He nuzzles into my neck, his voice muffled. "I don't care about work."

"Well, I do," I say, playfully elbowing him.

He responds by tightening his grip around my waist. "Technically, I'm the boss, so I can declare today a no-work day." He nibbles on my ear.

"Okay, *boss*, and what about all the work that won't get done today?"

But instead of answering, Aiden snakes a hand down my belly and in between my thighs.

I laugh in shock, but it's quickly cut off when he finds my center, rubbing gently against my clit. I suck in a breath. "Aiden," I breathe. "The time—"

"Shhhh," he whispers in my ear. "No one's gonna die if we're an hour late."

Chapter 18

Aiden

Lilly and I arrive at work around 9:30 a.m. The receptionist—Monica, I believe is her name?—definitely gives us a once over when we walk through the door together, and Lilly shoots her a look. From their interactions, I know they're friends. I wonder if she'll be honest with her about what's gone down between us.

I simply smirk and head off to my office. Lilly settles in across the hall from me, smoothing her hair as she often does. I find myself looking up from my desk, across the hall to hers, and catching her eye. God, I love the way she blushes so easily. Her cheeks turn this adorable pink color, and she bites her lip.

Shaking my head, I try to focus.

Later, my phone buzzes on the desk, and I look down to see a call from Asher.

"Hey," I answer.

"I've been meaning to check in with you about the foundation," he says, getting straight to the point.

"Aren't you supposed to be on a honeymoon?" I shoot back.

Asher chuckles. "They get cell service in the Bahamas, believe it or not. Olivia's at the spa, and I'm just hanging out by the pool. Thought it would be a good time to call."

I roll my eyes, laughing. "Your honeymoon is not a good time to call."

"How's the financial situation at the foundation?" Asher presses.

I snort. I glance up from my desk to see Olivia's office empty. She'd left a little while ago to supervise some workshop going on in one of the classrooms.

"It's decent. Could be better, but we've actually got a plan for that."

"A plan?" Asher echoes.

"Lilly wants the foundation to host art shows as fundraisers."

"Huh," Asher says. "It's a decent idea, actually. So you're implementing it?"

I nod. "Yep. We've been ironing out plans all week."

"That sounds great. So you think the foundation is worth keeping? It's not a lost cause?"

I smile. "Definitely worth keeping. No two ways about it."

"I trust your opinion on it," Asher says. "If you think it should stay, it stays."

"Thanks," I reply. "Now go hang out with your wife, you idiot."

We both hang up with a laugh.

Chapter 19

Lilly

I stare at myself in the floor-length mirror in my bedroom, turning from side to side to survey my outfit. The red dress I'm wearing falls just below my knees, the deep V showing off just enough cleavage to be sexy.

I take a deep breath. Aiden might not know what tonight will bring, but I certainly have an idea.

I've been thinking about it all week. I've been basically unable to think of anything else. After going over plans for the art show with him every day, I'd end up back at his apartment, wrapped in his arms and eventually seeing stars.

He'd suggested we go out Friday night, so here I am, dressed and ready for him to pick me up at my apartment. And while he's been nothing but a gentleman, only going as far as I'm comfortable and never asking for more, I've finally decided.

Tonight, I'm going to lose my virginity.

I'd mulled it over in my head every night this week. Part of me feels crazy. Am I just caught up in the moment? Falling for someone who's surely slept with more people than I ever will? Am I being stupid? But the way he cares for me, looks at me—it's got me unable to think straight.

Besides, isn't it time? At twenty-four, shouldn't I be doing this now?

And while my head might be telling me to wait, my heart is telling me something entirely different. That Aiden is more than just some guy. More than my last boyfriend or any boyfriend I've ever had. Aiden could be … it? I barely want to say it, to jinx it. And whether he's the one or not, he might just be the perfect one to lose it to.

A knock on my front door pulls me from my thoughts with a jolt, and I grab my purse and a jacket and hurry out of my room.

Aiden greets me when I open the door, looking me up and down and then smiling. "God, you look incredible," he says, leaning in to plant a soft kiss to my cheek.

"Thanks," I say with a grin, stepping out and shutting the door behind me.

Aiden drives us downtown. He'd mentioned a fun comedy club that he frequents with his brothers, and I'd agreed. We park nearby and walk a few blocks to the club, the brisk Seattle air chilly against my bare legs. Aiden wraps his arm around me as we walk, keeping me warm.

The show is good. We get drinks, and I find myself laughing hysterically at the comedians. At one point, Aiden rests his hand on my knee where it stays for the rest of the night. Even when I want to shift positions, I don't. I'd rather the warmth of his hand.

We walk back to his car hand in hand, and he asks if I want to spend the night again even though we both know the answer is yes.

When we get to his apartment, he offers me a drink, and I settle myself in on the couch like I've done every night this week. I've found myself feeling more at home here than in my own apartment.

Aiden joins me with our glasses of wine and pulls me against him in a cuddle.

"I liked the show," I say, taking a sip of my wine.

"I did too," Aiden says. He leans down to press a kiss on my head. "Want to know one of my favorite things about taking you out?"

I angle my face toward him. "What?"

"Getting to show you off. Especially when you look like this." He pinches the fabric of my red dress with his fingers.

I giggle, turning away from him.

"I'm serious," he says, nuzzling against me. "You're the prettiest girl in the world, and you let *me* take you out."

I smack him on the arm playfully.

He responds by planting a kiss on my neck. A kiss that turns into more kisses, and then his teeth are gently grazing my skin. I sigh, leaning back against him.

His arms wrap around me, grasping my breasts through the fabric of my dress and squeezing.

"Aiden, I …" I sigh as he continues trailing kisses down my neck.

I shift, turning so I can face him. He looks at me questioningly.

"I … I want you," I finally say.

His eyebrows furrow, and then he slowly understands what I mean. He looks at me in surprise. "Are you sure?" he asks.

I nod, running a hand along his chest. "I want you so badly, Aiden," I say again, gazing up into his eyes. "I want it to be you."

He smiles, reaching up to place a hand against my cheek, gently caressing me with his thumb. "You're sure?" he asks.

"Positive," I say, and I mean it. I really do. I'm ready.

Aiden presses his lips to mine. The kiss is soft at first but quickly becomes more passionate, and soon his tongue slips past my lips and tangles with my own. He wraps his arms around me, pressing me against his chest as he devours me.

I'm basically sitting on his lap so it's easy for him to scoop me up into his arms as he stands, his mouth still glued to mine. He carries me across the room and into his bedroom. He breaks our kiss and sets me down on my feet in front of the bed, leaving me breathless.

He reaches out to slowly slip the spaghetti strap of my dress over one shoulder, then does the same with the other. After a soft tug, the lightweight red dress falls, pooling around my ankles. He softly runs his hands around my bare waist, squeezing me gently. Then his hands slide up to the clasp of my bra, undoing it and pulling it free. He tosses it to the side. He takes a moment to stare down at my exposed breasts before grabbing the waistline of my panties and sliding them down my legs. I step out of them, leaving me completely and utterly nude.

Slowly scanning my body, Aiden takes a small step back and begins undressing. He unbuttons his shirt, removes his belt, then steps out of his pants. When he removes his underwear, I can see he's already hard.

While I've seen him naked before—hell, I've sucked his cock before—it's different this time. I'm taking in the size of him, suddenly unsure of whether he'll even fit inside of me.

As if sensing my nerves, Aiden spans the distance between us, placing his hands on either side of my face. "If you want to stop, just say so."

"I don't want to stop," I protest.

He smiles. "If you change your mind, tell me."

I nod.

Bracing me against him, he walks us backward toward the bed until the backs of my knees are resting against it. He nods toward it. "Lay back," he says.

I do, scrambling backward until I'm fully on the bed.

Aiden crawls over me, his gaze glued to mine. Then he leans down and presses a soft kiss to the flesh between my breasts. Looking up and meeting my gaze once again, he slowly presses kisses along my breasts, eventually reaching my nipple and taking it into his mouth. He sucks gently at first, then increases the pressure.

I sigh deeply, sinking into the bed below me.

He flicks my nipple a few times with his tongue before moving to my other breast, taking it in his mouth and sucking. He nibbles lightly, and I yelp in pleasure. He continues to suck and lick my breast, his free hand reaching up to gently massage the other one.

It isn't until I'm moaning and whimpering quietly that he finally stops and begins trailing kisses down my belly.

He spreads my legs and positions himself between them on the bed. Then he leans down to press a kiss to my knee, slowly placing kiss after kiss along my inner thigh.

I shiver in anticipation as he nears my center, growing more and more turned on.

Finally, he presses a kiss to my pussy and slowly licks along my slit. When he reaches my sensitive bud, I grasp the bed covers, moaning. He licks my clit a few times, working me up until I'm whining and shaking.

Then, sitting up, he takes a finger and presses it against my entrance. He slowly slides it inside of me, and I moan, shutting my eyes. He pumps it in and out of me a few times before inserting a second finger. He curls it against my g-spot, and I cry out, bucking my hips.

After a few moments of pumping, he slowly inserts a third finger. I feel myself stretching to accommodate it, but the fullness is unlike anything I've felt before. I open my mouth in a wordless cry, gripping the bedsheets.

"Does that feel good, baby?" he murmurs.

I nod.

He slowly pumps his fingers in and out of me, eventually picking up speed. He leans down toward me, still fingering me, to softly kiss my collarbone. "Are you ready for me, sweetheart?" he asks, raising his head to look in my eyes.

A small part of me panics. This is it. It's happening. But looking into Aiden's eyes, I know it's right. I nod. "Yes," I breathe. "Do you have …?"

He smiles. He slides off the bed, walking to his nightstand to pull a box out of the drawer. He grabs a condom out of it, opens it, and slides it on.

Then he crawls back on the bed and positions himself over me. I spread my legs, wrapping them around his waist. Resting on his elbows, Aiden stares down at me. "Ready?" he asks.

"Yes," I say with certainty.

He maneuvers himself a bit, and I feel him at my entrance. I tense in anticipation, a twinge of nerves rushing through me.

Aiden leans down to brush his lips against my ear, his breath warm on my skin. "Relax, sweetheart," he whispers, and then he slowly slides inside of me.

I gasp at the sensation of being stretched, at the twinge of pain. But slowly, I relax around him, getting used to the feeling of being filled. Aiden kisses my neck as he slowly pulls out and then back in.

I moan as he fills me for the second time, the pain replaced be sheer pleasure. I dig my nails into his back, holding onto him. I wrap my legs around his torso, desperate for more.

"Oh, Aiden," I breathe.

"Yeah, Lilly?" he asks as he slowly begins thrusting. "Does my cock feel good?"

I cry out in pleasure.

"You're such a good girl," he murmurs into my ear. "Taking my cock like this."

I whimper, both at the pleasure and at his words.

He picks up speed, and I grip him tighter. He snakes a hand down between us, finding my clit and rubbing.

I gasp, writhing beneath him. "Oh god, Aiden," I whimper.

He's panting, his breaths coming more ragged now. I can see the pleasure in his face, the way he sets his jaw, frowns as if he's almost in pain.

He rubs my clit faster, and I can feel my orgasm building. He pumps in and out of me, hitting my g-spot over and over again. The sensation is more than I can bear. My mouth open, I gasp and moan in absolute ecstasy.

"Aiden, I'm gonna come," I whimper.

"Good," he bites out, picking up speed.

My climax crashes through me, and I scream, digging my nails into Aiden's flesh as my legs shake around him.

He pumps just a few more times before finishing, collapsing on top of me, breathing heavily. With him still inside of me, I wrap my legs tighter around him, relishing the feeling of closeness as we catch our breaths.

Aiden lifts his head to smile down at me. "How was that?" he asks gently.

"Best sex of my life," I answer.

He laughs.

Chapter 20

Lilly

I bask in the afterglow for the rest of the evening. Aiden showers me with kisses before offering to make us popcorn for a movie, after which he wanders off to start it. I make my way to the bathroom to clean off, slipping into an old t-shirt of Aiden's that I find in his closet.

Walking back into the bedroom, I'm still in utter shock. How did this man completely turn my life upside down? Here I am, no longer a virgin and possibly even in ... love? I don't even want to admit it to myself yet.

I hop onto the bed, snuggling up in the covers. Aiden has a TV in his room, so I settle in and wait for him to return with the popcorn.

A buzz on the bed catches my attention, and I search the covers. Had I tossed my phone in here when I came in? When I find the offending phone, I realize it's Aiden's. A text from his brother, Asher, pops up on the screen.

Taking it in my hand, I begin inching off the bed. "Aiden," I call. "Your brother is texting."

But as my feet hit the floor, the screen swipes up, opening their text conversations. Without even meaning to, my eyes scan the texts. Asher is asking Aiden for an update on some email. But it isn't the newest text that catches my eye. It isn't even a text from Asher at all.

It's a text from Aiden. Something he'd sent Asher a few weeks ago. My blood runs cold, and I freeze to the spot.

Aiden: *Maybe I'll bring the program manager.*

Aiden: *You didn't warn me about how hot she is. All I can think about is getting in her pants.*

I swallow, staring down at the words on the screen that I don't want to believe are true. He's talking about me. Texting about me. To his brother. To Asher's credit, he shoots back a text that basically tells Aiden to shove it.

But …

I suddenly feel sick. I want to throw up. Oh my god. No. I didn't just …

Fuck.

All this time, I thought Aiden actually cared about me. But all he wanted was to simply "get in my pants." How could I have been so stupid? I'd known in my gut that Aiden was a player. I'd known from the second I'd laid eyes on him. And yet I'd allowed myself to get swept up in his games. And he'd gotten exactly what he wanted.

Anger, hurt, and humiliation all burn through me.

Suddenly unable to stand the thought of Aiden's t-shirt on my body, I pull it over my head, tossing it across the room. I grab my dress from the floor, pulling it back on.

Suddenly, the bedroom door swings open and in walks Aiden. He chuckles when he sees me. "You know, I have shirts you can borrow so you don't have to wear that to bed."

I turn to him, and he must read my expression because immediately his smile drops. "Lilly, what is it?"

"Was I just a game to you?" I ask, but the words come out quiet and choked.

"What—" I toss the phone at him, and he catches it, staring down at the screen—at the texts between him and Asher. "What are you—"

"*All I can think about is getting in her pants*," I repeat the text out loud, my voice even this time.

His gaze lands on the message, and his face falls. "Fuck." He looks up at me, his expression desperate, pleading. "Lilly, that's not—"

"It's not what?" I snap. "Real? You didn't send that? You didn't mean it? What?"

He swallows, opening his mouth, but no words come out.

"That's what I thought," I mumble, brushing past him and out the door.

I hurry into the living room, grabbing my purse off the kitchen counter and making my way to the door.

Aiden rushes after me. "Lilly, wait! Please don't go. Let me explain. It's not what it looks like."

"It's exactly what it looks like, Aiden!" I cry, twirling around. "You're a rich CEO who's used to getting whatever he wants, and I was just a stupid game to you. Well, congratulations. You won." Tears prick the corners of my eyes, but I hold them back.

"Please," he begs, reaching for me, but I yank my arm away.

"Fuck you," I mutter, slipping on my shoes and throwing open the front door. I slam it and run down the hallway before he has time to come after me. It isn't until I'm in the elevator that I let myself cry.

Chapter 21

Aiden

I don't think I've ever fucked up this badly. Or, at least, *felt* this badly about something I've fucked up.

I stare down at my phone in my hands. When Lilly had run out last night, I'd hesitated only a second before rushing after her. But she'd made it down to the lobby and was already hailing a cab by the time I managed to catch up to her.

I'd called her over and over again, but she didn't pick up. I'd gone to bed feeling sick.

I've spent all day calling and texting her. I just need a chance to explain myself. To explain how much of an asshole I was for sending that text. Because, honestly, that's the only excuse I have.

I shake my head, a fresh round of self-loathing washing over me. How could I have been so stupid? Why did I send that text to Asher all those weeks ago? What the hell was I thinking?

And why was I even thinking it in the first place? Obviously Lilly is the most beautiful girl I've ever seen, and obviously I wanted to sleep with her. But why the hell did I have to act like such a prick and pretend that that's the only thing about her that mattered? Because if I'm honest with myself, it was the only thing I cared about at the time. All I wanted *was* to get in her pants. And that's what makes this so hard.

Lilly wasn't wrong about me.

It's just that I've changed. The more time I spent with her, the more I realized that I cared about her. Liked her. Enjoyed her company. Even ... more?

But does it even matter now? Will she give me the chance to apologize?

I decide to take the weekend to let her cool down. Give her the time and space she obviously wants.

When Monday rolls around, I practically storm the Maria King Foundation in search of Lilly. She isn't there when I arrive, so I wait impatiently in my office, looking up every few seconds to see if she's settled in at her desk across the hall.

But she never comes.

I send her another text, asking her—pleading her—to talk with me, but she doesn't respond.

Tuesday is the same. I show up at work hoping to see her, and she never arrives.

Wednesday.

Thursday.

Friday, I ask the receptionist, Monica, if she's heard from Lilly.

"She's working from home this week, didn't she tell you?" Monica replies. "Says she has a cold or something."

I send a few more futile texts to Lilly, knowing she won't respond. And as much as I want to drive over to her apartment, bang on the door, and demand that she listen to me, I stop myself.

It isn't fair of me. Because, deep down, I know she's in the right. Whether or not I've grown doesn't change the fact that I started this relationship with bad intentions. And I need to respect what Lilly wants.

And at least for now, what she wants is seemingly not to see me.

I head home to my empty apartment for the weekend, thinking of the nights Lilly spent here. The left side of my bed feels cold and lonely. I've never felt that way after losing a girl. I was always ready to move on to the next.

But not now.

I make myself a strong drink, staring at my phone, hoping against hope that Lilly will text me back.

Chapter 22

Lilly

The missed calls and texts continue to roll in, and I continue to ignore them. Each buzz of my phone sends another wave of sadness through me, so I eventually lock it in my bedroom while I work on my laptop from the couch.

It's well past 5 on Friday night, but I've barely gotten any work done this week. Mostly what I've done is cried. Just thinking about it makes a lump form in my throat, but I swallow it, refusing to succumb to tears again.

I've never taken a breakup this hard before. If you could even call this a breakup. We were never official. We were never anything. And maybe that's what hurts so much. We were never anything. I was nothing to him.

And to me, he was so, so much more.

I'd had sex with him. The only person I've ever slept with, and he completely screwed me over.

It's not like I'm some prude who suddenly feels sullied or impure. And it's not like I was waiting for Mr. Right to give it up to. But the fact that he'd lied to me to get what he wanted—sex—and I'd so obliviously fallen for it is humiliating.

That's the emotion I keep coming back to. Humiliation. I'd given everything to him, exposed everything about myself. And to him, it was all a game.

I'd never really intended on staying home from work this week, but as each morning arrived, I just couldn't make myself go in. I couldn't make myself face him in person. The embarrassment, the hurt—it was all too much.

I'd called Monica to let her know I had a "cold" and wouldn't be coming in this week. Everything I normally do can be done from my laptop at home.

I can only hope that Aiden finishes up whatever loose ends he needs to and goes back to King Tech and I never have to see him again. The only problem is the art show next Thursday evening. We'd ironed out all the details last week, and most of the actual planning has been in his hands now. He's obviously going to be there, and I have to be there too. It was my original idea, after all. And I'm the program manager. I can't just not show up.

It's a fact I've been battling with all week.

It reminds me that I'm supposed to be helping him come up with the actual art pieces to display at the show. While I'd originally had grand plans of finding some local artists or showcasing a young student of the foundation, I decide that the various inventory we have at the building already—art from students and teachers that they donated or didn't want—will have to do.

I send Aiden a cordial, if not short, email about where to find these pieces and to simply choose whichever ones he thinks are best.

A sudden knock on my door startles me, and I look up from the couch. I feel a sinking sensation in the pit of my stomach. He wouldn't. He wouldn't actually come to my home demanding that I speak with him. Not after what he did. What he *knows* he's done.

I stand from the couch, smoothing my hair as I stalk across the room. I yank the door open, about to demand why he's there, when I see Monica standing on the other side.

My words fizzle on my tongue.

"You don't have a cold, do you?" she asks with a pointed look.

"Uh, I …"

"Oh, save it." She brushes past me into the apartment, and I mechanically shut the door behind her. When she reaches the living room, she twirls around, hands on her hips. "Something's going on with you and Aiden King."

I sigh, striding past her and settling back in on the couch. She sits beside me, expectant.

"We had a fling, and it's over," I say simply.

Her eyes widen. "You had a what?"

I close my eyes in frustration—not at her, but at me. At how stupid I was to allow myself to get caught up in all this.

"We kept seeing each other after his brother's wedding. I thought there was something real there, but apparently I was wrong."

Monica's eyebrows knit together in concern. "What made you realize that?"

"I saw a text from him to his brother basically saying that all he wanted to do was sleep with me."

Monica winces. "Oof. Yeah, that's not great."

"And I feel stupid and embarrassed, and I can't stand the thought of facing him at work," I admit.

Monica nods and is silent for a long moment. "You're sure he doesn't feel the same way about you?"

I widen my eyes at her. "I told you what I saw."

She purses her lips. "True. It's just that he's seemed completely not himself this whole week. He asked where you were—that's when I realized something was up. If you really were sick and your relationship with Aiden was strictly professional, you would have emailed him and told him yourself."

"He's probably acting weird because he feels bad. Or is worried this will somehow come back to bite him in the ass," I protest.

Monica shrugs. "Maybe. But he seems genuinely upset."

I think back to the myriad of text messages and missed phone calls from him. A few to save face would be expected, but dozens? That *could* mean he does actually feel sorry.

I lean back against the couch cushions, crossing my arms across my chest. "It doesn't change what I saw."

"Have you talked to him?"

I pause. "No."

She purses her lips. "I'm not saying he's in the right. But for your own peace of mind, it might be worth it to hear him out."

After a moment, I finally nod. She's probably right. It's the healthy thing to do. No matter how angry and humiliated I currently feel.

"But in the meantime," Monica says. "How about ice cream and a rom com?"

I smile.

Chapter 23

Lilly

While Monica's advice is sound, I find it easier said than done. When Monday rolls around, I still can't summon the courage to face Aiden. And as the days tick by, I realize that I'll *have* to see him Thursday night at the art showcase.

I've been fielding emails all week making sure the preparations are ready and things are set up. Most of it has fallen to Aiden, being more experienced with event planning and all that. I'd always envisioned myself more involved, but I suppose I hadn't envisioned my heart being broken right beforehand and absolutely hating Aiden King's guts.

The art show is being held at an event center downtown. It's one that King Tech has used on various occasions, apparently. That's what Aiden had said back when we were still on speaking terms.

I smooth my black dress over my thighs and glance at myself in the mirror. The dress is tight around the top and flares to just below my knees. My hair is pulled back in a low bun with a few pieces framing my face. But no matter how many times I fix something in my hair or switch out a piece of jewelry, nothing calms the butterflies in my stomach.

I'm seeing Aiden King tonight. The man who broke my heart.

In the most humiliating way possible, I might add.

A flash of anger courses through me, but I push it away. It's not going to help me now. I need to get through this event with grace and decorum, pretending like nothing is wrong. Aiden will eventually go back to King Tech, and I'll be left to continue my job—and hopefully these art shows. Everything will go back to normal.

I just have to get through tonight.

I take an Uber downtown to the event center. As soon as I step out of the car, those butterflies return with a vengeance.

The event center is nestled in the heart of downtown, with floor to ceiling windows giving a perfect view of the guests mingling inside. It looks like the perfect party.

I steel my nerves, grip my purse in my hand, and walk inside. Despite my turmoil of emotions, I'm overtaken by the joyful ambiance. The lighting is warm, soft string music plays, waiters pass by with trays of champagne, and the sound of conversation floats in the air.

I stand there in awe for a moment, taking it in. My idea. My idea for an art show that I'd only been dreaming about has become a reality. And a beautiful one, at that.

"Lilly!" A hand brushes my arm, and I turn to see Monica. She's beaming from ear to ear. "I had no idea, Lilly. Oh my god, why didn't you ever tell me?"

I stare back at her quizzically. "What are you talking about?"

Monica just shakes her head. She looks me in the eye, an expression of sincerity washing over her face. "They're gorgeous." Something catches her attention, and she notices a friend calling her from nearby. "I'll be back," she says, giving my arm a squeeze before disappearing into the crowd.

A waiter appears, offering me a glass of champagne. I accept, knowing a bit of liquid courage can only help get me through this night. Still puzzled by Monica's comment, I make my way through the room. Stands are positioned throughout the room, canvasses displayed on each. Most are facing inward, toward the crowd, so I can't see what Aiden has chosen until I'm nearing the center of the large room.

I smile in greeting at a few people I recognize—workshop teachers, foundation employees. They all seem to give me strange looks. I can't quite pinpoint what it is, but something seems ... different. Or am I just making it all up?

I lift my glass of champagne to my lips, about to take a sip, when my eyes land on the first painting I've seen displayed tonight. The glass hovers inches from my mouth, and then slowly, I lower it.

I stare at the painting in absolute shock. Almost as if on their own accord, my legs carry me closer until I'm standing just a few feet away from it.

The sweeping meadows, the vibrant skies. My name scrawled in the corner.

I turn slowly, surveying the rest of the paintings on display all around the room. My hand flies to my mouth in astonishment as I recognize each and every one.

These paintings are mine.

"Are you the artist?" a voice asks, pulling me from my racing thoughts.

I turn to see an older woman standing next to me. Her gray hair is pulled into a beautiful low bun. And her eyes match the dark blue dress she wears.

I can only nod in silent shock.

"They're beautiful," the woman compliments. She extends her hand. "My name is Lenore. I was close friends with Maria King."

"Lilly Richards," I introduce myself, shaking her hand. "I'm the program manager at the foundation."

Lenore smiles. "Maria would have loved these." She gestures to the paintings around the room. "You should be doing more with them. Aiden says you've never pursued this."

At a loss for words, I can only nod. Aiden has spoken with people about me?

"I have connections in Seattle, as well as other cities on the west coast." She reaches into her purse and pulls out a business card. She hands it to me. "Don't let your talent go to waste." With one last smile, she walks off, leaving me standing in absolute shock.

After gathering my senses, I turn and slowly start perusing the artwork. Obviously I recognize it all, but quickly I begin to realize where exactly I recognize it from. These are all paintings I'd left at the foundation. Things I'd done in my spare time, whether at work or at home, and hadn't deemed worthy enough to hang on my wall or give to friends.

More specifically, these are all paintings that had been in Aiden's office. It's where I'd stored most of them.

Just then, I catch a glimpse out of the corner of my eye of someone approaching me. I look up to see none other than Aiden King striding across the room toward me, his face a mask of apprehension and hope.

When he reaches me, he stands beside me, facing the painting I'm currently standing in front of.

I turn to meet his gaze. "You did this?" I ask quietly.

He nods. "Yeah." His eyebrows are crinkled in an emotion I can only describe as worry. "Do you like it?"

I laugh. I can't help myself. "Like it? I love it." I shake my head, suddenly overwhelmed. What Aiden has pulled together is nothing short of amazing. For me. "I can't believe you did this."

Relief floods his features, and he smiles. My stomach tightens. God, I'd missed his smile. "Choosing an artist for the showcase was easy once I realized the obvious choice was right in front of me." He laughs. "Literally. Sitting all around me in my office."

I smile, looking back at the painting, a swirl of emotions consuming me. I never would have done this on my own. I would never have sought out anything more for my art other than hanging on my walls, and I certainly never would have chosen myself for this art show. And Aiden knew that. So here is he, presenting my art to the elite of Seattle, and the business card of someone who could very well change my future is currently sitting in my purse.

"Thank you," I say quietly, despite the anger and hurt I still feel.

Aiden is silent for a moment. "I'm sorry, you know," he finally says.

I refuse to look at him. I'm afraid of my eyes welling up with tears if I do.

"Talk to me after the show?" he asks, gently placing a hand on my arm.

Still unable to look at him, I simply nod. I owe him that at least—to hear him out. And after this—all he's done—maybe there's something worth hearing after all. After a few seconds, he gently squeezes my arm and walks off.

Still in shock, I spend the rest of the evening mingling with attendees and foundation employees. Drinks and hors d'oeuvres are served, and after a little while, Aiden stands up to give a speech. He thanks everyone for coming, makes a few jokes, and finally, he turns to me.

My face reddens at the sudden attention while heads swivel toward me.

"I wanted to take a moment to discuss our artist tonight," he says with a smile. "Lilly Richards, if you aren't aware, is the talented woman who painted all these pieces you see displayed around us. As humble as she is, she would never have chosen herself to be the guest of honor here tonight. So that choice had to fall to me," he says with a laugh. "And I think you'll all agree it was a good choice." Murmurs of agreement filter through the crowd, and I look down at my feet with a smile. Aiden continues, "Not only is she a gifted painter, but she's the program manager at the Maria King Foundation—the reason it runs smoothly and continues to make a difference in our community."

Aiden pauses, glancing throughout the room, his gaze landing on mine for a brief moment. "My mom loved everything about art," he finally says. "Creating it, observing it, being in its presence. That was her life. That's what she cared about."

Just then, I notice Alec King off to the side, and I'm pleasantly surprised he showed up. Surely he's a busy man. As Aiden continues to talk about their mom, Alec simply nods along, his gaze glued to his younger brother.

"Me and my brothers have done a lot. We've been busy," Aiden says with a laugh. "But I think this foundation—this might be the thing I'm most proud of. It's certainly what Mom would have been the proudest of. She'd be happy to see what it does for the Seattle community in her name." Aiden takes a breath. Then that familiar smile returns to his face, and he looks back at the crowd again. "The foundation has plans to turn these art shows into a regular occurrence. So, thank you all for joining us tonight, and stay tuned for news on upcoming showcases." He holds his glass of champagne high. "To my mom, Maria King."

We all raise our glasses in a toast, and then the chatter in the room resumes. I watch Aiden walk over to Alec, the two of them quickly locked into a discussion which includes a hug.

I turn away, busying myself in the nearest conversation I can find between a few coworkers. Soon, I notice people beginning to filter out. I glance at the time on my phone—it's a little after nine.

Monica sidles up to me, giving me a side hug. "I'm going to head out," she says. "Again, beautiful work. Both your art and this whole thing." She gestures around us.

I smile. "Thank you."

She lowers her voice, glancing sideways. "Have you talked to Aiden?"

I shake my head. "No, but ... we're going to," I admit.

She nods, giving me a pointed look. "Hear him out. That's my vote. See you later." And with that, she leaves.

Most of the other foundation employees head out as well, saying goodnight to me before they do so.

It isn't long until the entire room has basically cleared out. It's just me, a couple attendees who are pulling on their coats, and Aiden and Alec, who are still talking. I'd head out myself if I hadn't promised Aiden I'd speak with him.

I shuffle nervously, biting my lip and staring up at one of my paintings. It's then that they both notice me. Aiden says something to Alec, and after a clap on the back, they part ways, Alec heading for the door.

Aiden approaches me. He stands next to me, his hands in his pockets, silent for a moment. "I think the event went well, overall," he finally says.

I nod. "I think so too." I glance around, then laugh. "I still can't believe …" I trail off.

He smiles. "A few people expressed interest in buying some of your pieces. I obviously didn't want to agree before talking with you."

I raise my eyebrows in surprise. "Really?"

"Really. And I know they'd pay whatever you ask for them."

"I—yes, I guess." I laugh. "Wow. I don't even know what I'd price them at …"

"You can take time to think it over," Aiden assures me.

We stand in silence for a moment, the weight of the last couple weeks seeming to settle on our shoulders.

"Lilly, I'm sorry." He says it quietly without looking at me. He's staring down at his shoes, his hands still in his pockets. His eyebrows are drawn together in frustration. "I don't have an excuse for the text messages you saw. I was a complete ass, and that's it."

I'm shocked at his honesty, at his willingness to admit it.

He looks up from the floor, meeting my gaze. "But I have to tell you that that text was sent before I got to know you. Before we spent time together, before the wedding, the dates we went on, before …" He swallows, clenching his fists. "Lilly, I can't even begin to tell you how sorry I am for how you must have felt after seeing that. It was real to me, I swear it was."

I'm at a loss for words.

"And if you don't believe me, or forgive me, I understand. But I needed to tell you. I couldn't live with myself without telling you." He runs a hand through his hair, taking a deep breath. "I'm in love with you, Lilly. I spend every second thinking about you. Your smile, your laugh, the way you tease me, drive me crazy. I was an idiot to think that you were any less than … than the woman of my dreams."

I stare at him for a long moment, and as the seconds tick by, I can see the hope slowly fading from his face. "You … love me?" I repeat. It's the only thing I can manage to utter.

"I love you," he echoes.

Tears spring to my eyes, and I don't have the willpower to hold them back. I rerun our last night together in my mind—how I'd felt reading that text, how I'd run from his apartment, how I'd cried for days.

But then I think of the art show. How he'd chosen my paintings, lovingly curated them, talked about me in his speech. And now. He *loves* me.

"I love you too," I whisper, a tear sliding down my cheek.

A desperate sigh of relief escapes him, and before I have time to say or do anything, he's closed the distance between us and wrapped me in his arms. He squeezes tightly, nestling his face against my neck. "You mean it?" he murmurs into my ear.

I nod against him. "Yes."

He squeezes tighter, breathing in deeply. Then he lets go, planting a soft kiss to my cheek before leaning back to look me in the eyes. He puts a hand on either side of my face, gently wiping a tear away with his thumb. "I love you," he says again, a wide grin breaking out across his face.

Utter joy bubbles up within me, and I laugh, reaching for his face and pulling him to me in a kiss. The kiss is soft and sweet at first, his lips gently moving against mine. Then it becomes harder, faster, desperate, his fingers intertwining in my hair.

I grip his dress shirt in my fingers, pulling him closer. I *need* him closer. I need him. Now.

Aiden briefly breaks the kiss to glance around. I do too. The room is empty. The building is empty. We're the only two here. He bites his lip, smirking down at me. That smirk that makes my knees go weak.

He reaches down, underneath my skirt, finding my center through my panties and rubbing gently. I moan softly, and he covers my mouth with his, kissing me deeply as he continues gently rubbing me. When he reaches a finger underneath my panties to slide it against my slit, I break our kiss with a gasp of pleasure.

Aiden smiles down at me. "You like that?"

I nod.

He slowly slides his finger from my bud, along my slit, stopping at my entrance. Then he slips his finger inside of me. I throw my head back with a deep moan, bucking my hips against him. He kisses my neck, down my collarbone, my chest, to the tops of my breasts.

He pumps his finger in and out of me, and I whimper softly. "Aiden," I whine.

"Yeah, baby?" he asks.

"I want *you*." I open my eyes to meet his gaze, my own desire mirrored there. "I want you inside of me."

His gaze darkens, and his jaw tightens. His hand disappears from under my skirt. He grabs my arm, pulling me across the room to the nearest wall. He pulls out his wallet, fumbling for a condom. Then he unzips his pants, pulling his cock free and sliding it on.

Then he gently guides me until my back is against the wall. He reaches down to grab my thighs, hoisting me up and then pinning me against the wall with his body. I gasp in surprise.

"Wrap your legs around me," he orders. "And hold onto me."

I do as he says, wrapping my legs tightly around his torso and wrapping my arms around his neck. He presses his lips to mine in a desperate kiss, a kiss that leaves me breathless. Then he reaches down between us, finding my panties and sliding them aside. He nestles closer to me, and I can feel him against my entrance. He looks back to me, his eyes glued to mine, and then he enters me.

I gasp in pleasure, my nails digging into his back. He sighs deeply, still holding my gaze. "Does that feel good?" he asks.

I nod. Just like last time, there's a slight twinge of discomfort, but it's immediately replaced by an overwhelming sensation of pleasure.

Aiden slowly pumps in and out of me, almost agonizingly so. I moan, gripping him tighter against me.

"God, you feel so good," he murmurs in my ear. His hands under my thighs, holding me up, his fingers dig into my flesh, driving me wild.

He picks up speed, thrusting faster and faster. My moans are becoming louder, echoing off the walls of the large room. His hand reaches between us, finding my clit and rubbing. I shriek at the sensation, gripping him tighter.

The pleasure is building and building—I can feel myself getting closer to the edge.

"Aiden," I whimper.

He covers my mouth with his, his tongue dancing with mine, devouring me. The kiss is desperate, taking all of me, leaving nothing.

I whimper into his mouth as the pressure at my core builds.

He breaks the kiss to murmur, "Come for me, Lilly. Be my good girl and come for me."

At that, I crash over the edge, gasping. Aiden isn't far behind, and when he pulls out, he sets me back on my feet. We lean against each other, panting, our hands intertwined. I look up to see that devilish smirk on his face. That stupid smirk that gives me equal parts irritation and desire. Only this time, I see much more behind that smile. I see love.

He reaches out to brush a strand of hair behind my ear. "I love you, Lilly Richards," he says with a smile I can only describe as giddy.

"I love you, Aiden King."

Penelope Ryan

Penelope Ryan writes sizzling hot romances with dominant men and lots of dirty talk and spice.

Read the next book in the Billionaire Brothers series, *The Billionaire's Wife* Stay (starring Alec King):

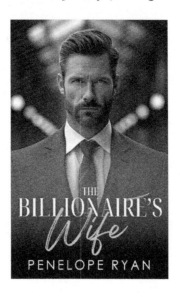

Books by Penelope Ryan:

The Billionaire's Assistant

The Billionaire's Obsession

The Billionaire's Wife

My Best Friend's Billionaire Brother

Tempting the Billionaire

Teacher's Pet

Losing It

The Arrangement

Small Town Billionaire

Hi!

Did you enjoy the book?

Authors and readers depend on reviews. If you enjoyed the book, please consider leaving a review. Thank you so much!

Printed in Great Britain
by Amazon